THE PHOENIX

Or misrule in the land of Nod

by Onyeka

To Kairo

The future belongs to those
who prepare for it today
Peace and many blessings
from Nzingha x-x
Dec 2015

ISBN - 0- 9533182-7-3

Printed in London U.K.

Cover, 'The Phoenix Risen,' by Coral
Cover photograph by Daniel
Layout by Atyeni
Production by Narrative Eye
Photograph 'Contemplation,' by George West
Editing by Alistair

Website: www.onyeka.co.uk
Email: thinktank_27@yahoo.com

**The Phoenix
or
Misrule in the land of Nod**

Being the third and final part of Waiting to Explode

Acknowledgments:

To the creator known by many names and all of those who
fight against injustice, to all the organisations and community
groups, let freedom reign.

In Loving memory of

Baba John Henrik Clarke
Baba Ishakamusa Barashango
Baba Kalendar
Baba Del Jones
Baba Asa Hilliard
Baba Amos Wilson
Deng Ajak

Preface

"So few of us can understand what it takes to make a man - the man who will never say die; the man who will never give up; the man who will never depend upon others to do for him what he ought to do for himself; the man who will not blame God, who will not blame Nature, who will not blame Fate for his condition; but the man who will go out and make conditions to suit himself. Oh, how disgusting life becomes when on every hand you hear people (who bear your image, who bear your resemblance) telling you that they cannot make it, that Fate is against them, that they cannot get a chance."

The Most Honourable

Introduction

This is the third and final part of Waiting to Explode and the sequel to the Black Prince. It has been a long time coming. To be honest I'm glad it's done! At last Tayo, Flex and Michael can sleep! But the Phoenix stands alone, even if you don't have knowledge of the previous two. (But when you've read this book, I suggest you go back and read the rest for a deeper understanding.)

When you do read this book try not to presume. Do not presume this is a straight narrative devoid of deeper meaning. There is significance lurking under the surface and present in the core. This book will unfold differently each time you read it.

Is this book controversial or offensive? Is it the camera's picture which is the offence? Or the starving child that it films? Or is the offence the fact that anyone in this world should be starving at all!

Living in England and being unwanted, is a feeling of being an aborted representation or the one that escaped the flawed plan of eugenics. To be, to exist at all, is itself controversial - when everything in the fabric of the culture is denying you, reviling you and at the same time conversely ignoring you. But the time is long gone when one cries to be heard. These are words written not for your sympathy or acknowledgment, but are a statement of being.

So see how you love it, not like it. I don't expect you to be neutral. There is no such thing as neutrality and since there isn't, don't claim it! Come with your prejudices, read and see what happens to them along this journey.

But don't do this book the disservice of skim reading it, avariciously flicking through a few pages and thinking you can get a feel for it. Don't play yourself or this writer short! Experience it complete or not at all. When you've read it for the first time, I suggest you might like to read it again, just in case. You never know, you might have missed something.

I'll not say anymore.

But yes we exist and can speak, but whether you listen is a matter for you and your conscience.

Onyeka

Ten little n. boys

Ten little n.. boys went out to dine;
One choked his little self and then there were nine.

Nine little n.. boys sat up very late;
One overslept himself and then there were eight.

Eight little n.. boys travelling in Devon;
One said he'd stay there and then there were seven.

Seven little n.. boys chopping up sticks;
One chopped himself in half and then there were six.

Six little n.. boys playing with a hive;
A bumble bee stung one and then there were five.

Five little n.. boys going in for law;
One got in Chancery and then there were four.

Four little n.. boys going out to sea;
A red herring swallowed one and then there were three.

Three little n.. boys walking in the zoo;
A big dog ate one and then there were two.

Two little n.. boys sitting in the sun;
One got frizzled up and then there was one.

One little n.. boy left all alone;
He went and hanged himself and then there were none.

Yet
See the Phoenix rising from the ashes.
Dead but now reborn in light,
Blinding the world with light.

Kwame Aja

Autumn 1992

"Do you mean black power? God made us all equal," Kwame Aja replied assertively. He was a pensive rather toady little youth who looked just like a weasel.

"Maybe?" Tayo Akinjo said, "But I'm saying God helps those who help themselves. Listen are you still jealous because of what happened in the election? We were students then. Come on you know how to make money. We could do something good together. We both know what's happening don't we?"

"No. Don't presume! I mean - I've got white people in my family. Look the Ajas, that's my name, are mostly Creoles. You can find them in Ghana and Nigeria. There's a lot of white in my family!!?"

"I didn't ask about your family! I asked about you!"

"Oh I'm tired of this. I've got too much to do! I'll be working in the city next year with Venture plc."

"Venture, don't you know the history of that organisation?" Tayo was genuinely shocked.

"I know they helped finance slavery in America. I don't care so long as they're good to me. Don't you see! You're trying to stop me already."

Their conversation was interrupted - a tramp, with blonde bushy hair, eyebrows and a beard like Father Christmas (Old Nick), drunk and bemused, staggered towards them through the twilight. His eyes were the bluest of blue and he stunk like he had just died.

Kwame was beside himself with joy, "I shouldn't say this - I shouldn't say this," he said, staring at the tramp as he dribbled down his chin, "but that man looks just like **our** saviour!"

Tayo bit his lip so hard it bled and had to refrain from impulsively slapping some sense into him, "your saviour not mine," he rumbled, "your saviour not mine!"

"Now you're getting rude!" Kwame interrupted, agitated, but watching in exaltation, as the tramp disappeared down the subway. Kwame stepped away and turned his back on Tayo, whose fists were clenching.

The sun died into evening. The wind picked up the leaves and litter, scattering them over the metropolis of London.

Kwame turned back and looked at Tayo's fists and changed his approach, "Listen have a nice life, let's talk another time. You're a smart guy. You've got a couple of degrees. Why don't you do something with them?"

"I am. I will." Tayo said, looking at his bus as it whizzed passed his stop and realising he would have to wait twenty minutes for the next. He also noticed that a small group of people had become curiously interested in their conversation.

"Listen, take care," Kwame said shaking Tayo's hand, "we can't all be the same. You live your life and I'll live mine." Kwame scurried off, clutching his briefcase like a new pupil at an elite public school.

Tayo Akinjo frowned, adjusted his pouch, pulled the hood of his jacket up over his head and thought, 'it's brother this and brother that and brother how's your soul, but its the thin black line of heroes that make the wheel begin to turn. So many

Negroes, so few Africans.'

And it rained grey-grey rain and it rained grey rain everywhere and on every living thing.

Karibu! nyumba

A vacant plot on a hill overlooking the metropolis of South London with a sign marked, 'Ready for development.' It was a shell worn to its husk, drenched dry by over a **decade** of arid rain and wet sun, dripping with autumn leaves. The liquid moisture of the morning dew, wooden timber frames rotten to the core... almost. The stone foundations decaying - not destroyed.

The evening drew onto night and the moon and stars shone bright. An owl shrieked. A mouse scurried across the floor, a crisp packet landed unceremoniously on the wooden slates, drifted, floated, blown by the wind and finally plummeted through the open gaping wound and into the basement below.

Shattered glass and jagged window frames gashed wide, with nails rusted in and twisted brown. A dead rat and a broken mirror caked in slime and filth. The front door twisting on it's broken hinges. Broken slates and tiles lying in heaps around the garden. Here part of the roof in tact, there a part missing.

Parts of a dustbin, coke cans, bottles of Smirnoff and Southern Comfort littering the floors, remnants of a fish and chip dinner, rat droppings and buzzing flies. The whirl of a broken spinning fan being driven relentlessly, back and forth, by the blowing wind.

But the Sun was breaking through the trees and sending a light show through the encircling foliage. The earth was still wet with morning dew and the vine creepers had crept over brick, stone and glass. Magpies all black in the morning cooed like doves flitting to and fro, to feed their ever-growing nests. Even the sliver-foil from cast off Kit-Kat wrappers were twisted into their dangling homes, perched precariously at the pinnacle of red brick outcrops.

But days went by and time marches on. Thirteen years. Yet still no love, only the magpies keeping custody from their treetop nests.

Banks and broads

The winter of 2005

The streets were wet with tears, wetting a thousand cheeks from a thousand eyes, from a thousand mothers. Tears staining blood red, illuminating the cracks between the pavements, like the veins on a burnt man's skin. The politicians lied and the mother's cried. Five thousand brothers and sisters killed, by five thousand more, on a hundred streets, yet the silence was ghastly, still, pale. Like an apparition seen just before dawn. And the clowns laughed as the brothers died, short spring for such a long winter. A generation wiped out by the misogynistic-misanthropy of a nation that cares more for its cats and dogs, than its citizens darker than blue. And the angels lost their wings, as the saints swapped sides and the prophets all told lies! Who wants to hear the truth? It's more fun to be on the devil's side, than be righteous in an unrighteous time.

'The winter of 2005 is the best ever. I've earned more money this month than the whole of last year,' Tayo Akinjo thought, standing in '**his**' bank, adjusting **his** Versace shirt and waistcoat and tightening **his** Gucci tie.

Tayo looked at his expanding girth and his expanding bank account, as he thumbed through the pages of his statement. Outside the rain came down hard, splashing water horizontal onto the windowpane. Businessmen and shoppers were soaked, as they bustled through the city streets. 'Never come out in England without a jacket,' Tayo thought grinning... then he stopped. 'A cat is being killed by a dog,' he brooded and shuddered, as the feeling infected his spirit.

"When will I get to see one of those cashiers? I've only got half an hour," Tayo muttered, using the left side of his brain to gain control of himself and simultaneously looking at the queue.

Tayo Akinjo should have been happy. He was a successful venture capitalist. He had a whiz for making money, he could smell a deal a thousand miles away.

"Cashier number 4 please," the electronic tannoy announced and Tayo woke from his meditation.

'At last a free counter,' Tayo thought, adjusting his tie again.

He smiled a gregarious smile, as he stepped one foot closer to the cashier counter.

'Oh no! I hope it's not her,' he thought and checked his watch again. 'Every week it's that same stupid girl, (cashier number 1 Suzie).'

"Cashier number 2 please."

But Suzie couldn't help being stupid. She had come from Doncaster to London to PARTY! That meant beer, Guys, Football. Yeah, she was a fully qualified **ladette**, tattoos, short skirt, plunging neckline. She had been going steady with Mark Braithwaite a market stall holder in Elephant and Castle, but that didn't mean that she couldn't shag others, 'three this week,' she thought 'and always safe sex.'

"Cashier number 3 please."

Well, if you call asking their name first, safe and she wasn't prejudiced, prejudice never entered her mind. "So long as they're not Pakis, have fit bodies, big dicks and can move well, he can be my fuck buddy," she always told her friends, much to their amusement. She wore the most revealing dresses she could get away with and my, she could get away with a lot! She could suck a plum from a peach! She had been out on the raze last night and she was half falling asleep at the counter - but

then she saw Tayo coming, she could almost smell his
Africaness and she liked it, she wanted it. 'At last it's him
again!' she thought, adjusting her top, so the top of her breasts
almost popped out.

'Oh my God,' Tayo thought, 'who does she think she is?' And he
watched her disgusted, 'oh don't say it! Not again!'

"Cashier number 1 please."

Tayo frowned.

Suzie smiled.

Tayo sighed.

Suzie adjusted her top again.

Her breast flopped out. She pretended not to notice and Tayo
looked straight ahead as he walked to the counter. The whole
bank was watching, but with their English reserve they were
pretending not to.

Suzie stared at Tayo wanting him to look at her pink areola and
the pale white mammary around. She wanted him to look at her
pride and joy that men had fought in two cities for, but Tayo
was cold.

'Yes I've got seven hundred pounds to put in,' Tayo said
confidently.

"Anything else?" Suzie asked, staring at him and sticking her
nipple out.

"Yes and I would like to withdraw fifty pounds, I've got my
cheque book here."

"Anything else!"

"No that's all." Tayo didn't even smile.

Suzie went red, bright red, adjusting her top and doing up her button. Rage and embarrassment overwhelmed her, 'I'm not good enough for him? Right!!!' she thought.

"I'm afraid, I'm going to need your passport and two proofs of address, before I can let you take money out," she said smiling.

"What do you mean?" Tayo replied, "I come in here at least three times a week, I've been coming here for at least four years. In fact, this has been my bank longer than you have been employed here!" He bit his lip.

"Sorry," Suzie said, "I don't know you, sorry.... Now if I knew you? I could let you take the money. But...."

"It's alright. I'll go to another branch... no wait a minute, this is wrong!! Can I speak to the manager please?!"

"As you wish Mr.. Ak..in..jo, just wait here?

Tayo stared at the floor, and tapped his foot. The heel of his shoe clinked on the marble. 'Marble floor, in a bank! That's where my bank charges are going, typical.' Tayo stared behind him. A long line of irate customers stared back. Tayo scowled and almost thought he was ten years younger. But then he remembered he wasn't.

It took an hour and a half of arguments and crossed forearms with furrowed brows, before Tayo got his money. He was only two hours late for work and Mary 'his' boss, was standing at the door looking at her watch.

Mary

Mary, that unmarried mother inferior, an emaciated middle class, middle of the road, pot smoking Islington liberal. Mary prided herself on her black admirers and insisted on free love, so long as she was in control of the freedom! She had the Audrey Hepburn look but with none of the Oscar winning ability. She ran three miles a day to keep herself trim and it worked. She was a stick insect in clothes! But her feminine qualities had leaked out somewhere. Spiritually trans-gendered. Her face plain and pasty, with no redeeming qualities, not eyes, not mouth, not nose. She grew her hair long, far too long to be perceptibly practical. She would waft it across her face every five minutes, like one of those models on a cat walk and fawn like she was on TV. But she wasn't!

Mary smelt wonderfully of dried sperm, alcohol and marijuana. She fancied herself the real bohemian, despite the fact she worked fifteen hours a day. Weekends were her release! Yes every weekend she got stoned and sexed out of her mind. There was never a shortage of black bucks to satisfy her. That's how she liked them. Young, big, strong, dumb and full of cum - until she had finished with them! After all, she was still young at heart. Only fifty-five! "There's a lot of life left in the old dog yet," she could be heard to say! And there was. She had drained it out of everyone else!

Tayo was late.

"You're late," Mary mumbled, as Tayo eventually stumbled up the stairs and he was soaked with rain.

"I know I'm late." Tayo replied, shaking the rain off his coat and accidentally catching her. She scowled. He frowned without apologising and remembered just for a moment who he was, "so are you my mother!!?" he growled, unrelenting, unremorseful and implacably defiant.

Thirty-four years earlier.

Tayo's Mum

She had all the auspices of a working class mentality. Fag in mouth and chip butties for breakfast. Chip-pan-grease-pie and sugar filled dumplings, "that's what they like. Get that down yah, ya screaming mite." She looked and acted like a character from a Dickensian novel. Mrs Fagin should have been her name, but culture wasn't her game.

"I can't be bothered with reading and all that," she said. "That's for folks that don't have 'nathing' to do. Book work. I'd rather have bed werk!" She'd picked up some useful patois from her numerous black clients. She was very familiar with black isms and skisms. "Poor little black mites. Parents abandoned ya have they. It's alright! Auntie Mel will look after ya! Poor little blighters! All alone in the world," she would mutter.

The year was 1971 December 29th. Auntie Mel's business was twenty years old, when Mr and Mrs Akinjo rang her doorbell. It chimed and then stopped, turning into a brief discordant noise, before petering out. She meant to fix it, but somehow she had never found the time.

The sun had been shining all day, but now the evening cloud had soaked up all the warmth. The wind picked up and the moon was out, white, cold and pale, certainly there was no mother's love there.

Mr Akinjo was stern and arrogant in a white tie, blue suit (Otis Redding style), and slip on shiny shoes, with a side parting like Sidney Poitier. Mrs Akinjo aggressive and a little dominant, a long dress and shawl, gloves and **hate**. She looked like an every day 1970's/1960's style Nigerian migrant, who was trying not to look, like an everyday ordinary Nigerian migrant!

'They don't look destitute to me.' Auntie Mel thought, looking them up and down. 'He looks like a tax collector and she looks like she works in some hospital,' and she was right.

Mr Akinjo peered at Auntie Mel and took off his glasses, rubbing the lenses.

"This is my son," he said almost proudly, with a strong Yoruba accent, there was a trace of defiance. (Strange emotions when one considers his next action.)

"Take him, you look after him. We can't keep him. Take him."

Auntie Mel looked at him with blue suspicious eyes.

"But I don't even know your name. You don't know mine."

"Your name's Melanie Simmons isn't it? We saw it in the advert in the paper. You run this place," he peered into her front room.

"Why don't you come in?"

"No," he said, "We don't have time."

"What's the matter, are you in some sort of trouble? What's the hurry?"

"No hurry. I just don't believe in wasting time."

"But this is your son, don't you want to know something about me?"

"Listen my name is Mr Akinjo, this is Tayo Akinjo, (pointing to the baby) this is my wife. We're from Nigeria."

"What part of Jamaica is Nigeria in?" Mel blurted, finishing the stub of her cigarette.

"Jamaica?" Mrs Akinjo spat ignorantly, "we're not Jamo, we're not cotton picking slaves, we're Africans!"

Mel looked at them blankly. 'It's all the same to me,' she thought.

"Listen, do you want money, we've got no money. You look after the child. Please," Mr Akinjo said.

"But tell me why? Do you work?"

He nodded.

"And are you working?"

"Yes," Mrs Akinjo replied annoyed.

"Then why?"

"You know why? Think about it. This is your country not mine. You think about it."

"I don't understand?"

"Look you know everywhere you go they put up the sign, no blacks, no dogs, no Irish. Look we're black!" he showed her his hand, almost ridiculously to confirm it. "We can't get anywhere decent. We stay in one room. That's not right. I don't want that for my son. We walked up your front garden, it's massive. All the gardens on this street are massive. I mean, when we think of England back home, this is the kind of place we think of, white fences, green lawn. I mean look at your house it's enormous, eight bedrooms. That's probably why you decided to take up fostering. I expect your husband's dead and you're all alone.

All of your children are grown up?"

Auntie Mel nodded.

"You see I know everything about you." He said. "Just look after my son. You won't teach him to do that?" he added, staring at the cigarette butts.

"Not unless he want's to!"

"Please he's my son," Mrs Akinjo added!

"Then you look after him." Mel retorted, "I run a clean house, I've got six other children. They're all looked after. (Her cockney accent always came out when she got angry). Just don't tell me how to do my job Mr and Mrs Akiiijoe!"

"Akinjo."

"Whatever! Just don't tell me how to do my job! I know what I'm doing. I brought up two generations of children and they're all the same under the skin! Keep them warm, feed them, keep them clean."

Mrs Akinjo nodded. "Take him," handing over the bundle of nappy, blanket, woolly hat, pink shawl, baby and all.

Auntie Mel grabbed him in both arms, and coughed a little smoke in his face.

He cried.

"Darling don't cry. I'm your mummy now," Auntie Mel said and smiled at the Akinjos.

Eventually the door was shut. Mr and Mrs Akinjo left the same way they came. Mrs Akinjo stopped midway down the path, turned back, almost as if she changed her mind. But a wind came up from the West and blew her doubts away. She sighed to herself and walked on. Within half an hour they were far-far away.

Auntie Mel smiled, as she stubbed a cigarette out on baby Tayo's hands. He cried.

"You're my little nigger now. Stop crying!" she said. And she slapped him until his face and body was bruised raw.

But he didn't stop crying for fifteen years. Called nigger 89,603 times!! Cake and biscuits, roast beef and Yorkshire pudding. Fish and chips and black pudding. Toad in the hole and apple crumble with custard. Roast pork and crackling, rhubarb and apple turnovers. No patti, roti, rice and peas, yam, fried plantain, sweet potato, powdered yam or Egusi stew, garri, moi moi, ackee or saltfish. And no Christmas card from his mother - let alone one for Kwanzaa.

When he could walk, he would fight, when he was old enough to step outside the door he did, and he never looked back. But he often looked forward.

'Fashion, was it nothing but fashion?' Tayo often thought, in the midst of contemplation, 'giving your children away, was it nothing but fashion!' He could still see the cigarette burns on his hands, in the half light of a full moon. But he often fooled himself into believing that he couldn't. 'They could have managed. Why did so many Africans give away their children? We were nothing but slaves, playthings, curiosities, nothings changed.'

Tayo's Mum II

December 31 2005

She sat her arms folded grandmother style around her Bible and
she smiled with resignation, resignation to the reality of life.
Feet up in front of the inane, insane drivel of daytime soaps:
the goggle box was on full blast. But Mrs Akinjo flitted in
and out of sleep.

Tayo flicked the lock and stepped into the porch. Shutting the
door behind him. He kissed his mum on the cheek, "How you
doing. I brought you some more books."

"Oh son," she said, sleepily stirring from her slumber, "my
darling, I didn't here you come in."

"Yeah too much wine mother," Tayo said, taking off his shoes,
"as I was saying, I've got some books for you."

"You know," slowly waking, "I've got no time for any books
except the Bible."

Tayo kissed his teeth, "I love you, but I don't believe you. I
can't follow you, won't follow you. But I love you."

"What do you mean?"

"Never mind." Tayo said, taking off his shoes.

"Have you heard from uncle? Have you told him I don't ever
want to see him in this house!"

"What do you mean, this is my house son."

"So it is, but do you really want to be associating with a man who is into that business!"

"Uncle is a good man, he looks after his family and his wife has a new Benz every year."

"Yeah and he's screwing every woman in town. I'm sure he's a pimp!"

"A son shouldn't talk like that in front of his mother!"

"No disrespect mother," Tayo said, "But I am thirty-five years old. When am I going to be old enough to have an adult conversation with you? Besides that's the point, I was a man when I met you and I'm more of a man now."

"I know that but I wish sometimes you did more of the things that other sons do."

"Really, like what? Buy perfumes and things. All that frivolous materialism! Yes and going back to my original subject, I know he's not my **real uncle**! And I know he has a wife."

"I don't want to talk about it."

"Yeah I bet you don't, but anyway have you spoken to father recently?"

"I can't talk now."

"Really you should call or visit him or something. He's still your husband isn't he? And he's the father of your son standing here."

"If you've come here to lecture me you might as well go. I've got such a headache!"

"You're always the same whenever we get deep. You always
want to change the subject, or your head hurts. That's the
problem with our culture, we 're always burying things under
the sand and hoping they'll go away. But they won't. We tried
to bury slavery, racism, colonialism and you tried to bury what
you both did to your son and what you're doing now to your
husband. No let's expose it for what it is, in all its sinister
corruption."

"If you hate our culture so much, why don't you just live and
die like an oyibo!"

Tayo laughed. "But mother dear I am an oyibo and whose fault
is that? Don't give your children to white people to look after
and expect them to come back your willing slaves!"

"Oh you're so ungrateful!"

"Ungrateful!" Tayo said, "remember it was me that found you,
not the other way round. You left me to rot!"

"It wasn't like that. Every family in Nigeria..."

"Don't say it. Just because everybody's doing it - it doesn't
make it right! But what I'm saying is that if I can make peace.
You can make peace with father."

"I don't know?"

"I do! So he's a drunkard, so he's whored his way across the
city. I'm not asking you to sleep with him! I know who you're
with (and he's not much better and he's married too.) But all I'm
asking you to do is make peace with him. That's all. Will you
think about it?"

"Okay," she said wearily, "Do you want some jollof rice?"

"No it's okay you rest. I ate before I came," Tayo said, catching
his breath and finally getting the inner peace to smile at her. He
should have been thinking how to make up for lost years. But
he had long put aside the idea of the ideal African family.

'I know my family and I love my family,' he thought, staring at
his mother and the picture of his father, 'because I want to end
the destructive cycle of fracture and separation. And that is the
only reason!' And he thought of a red sun on a green land
with black thoughts and he sighed a little, when he thought
about how respectable he had become.

Tayo cleared away the empty cup and washed it. His mother
was already asleep. He kissed her forehead and left a hundred
pounds in an envelope on the table.

He shut the door behind him and stepped out onto the street.
'I'll take the bus back,' he thought. He had left his car on the
outskirts of the congestion zone. "Yeah I'll get the bus back," he
said out loud.

January 2006

The new year slapped the World on it's face and sent it spinning. But there was no fanfare. The winter of 2005 just passed into the winter of 2006 like each new year was a big joke, but nobody was laughing.

But something spiritual, a big bang had just happened! It was good the gloves were off, now you could see the naked closed fist beneath.

"I don't have anything against blacks, some of my best friends are blacks, but....."

"I don't see why it's always the proper (white) British who should be put last."

"Yeah I'm proud to be English, what's wrong with that. I don't see why I should have to keep apologising for who I am. I've got rights too!"

"I don't have anything against that lot...but whose going to stick up for me!"

"Everybody knows that they bring in the diseases."

"I don't mind the Polish, the Australians and that, because after a few generations you won't even notice where they had come from. But all these blacks and Asians, whether they're born here or not.....we'll...."

"I'm not racist, but..."

"I'm not ....a racist but..."

"I'm not a racist... but"

2006 the growth of the far right, the end of political correctness, immigration and racism at the top of the political agenda - but where was Tayo? Shining his shoes and picking the dirt from his manicured finger nails, straightening his tie and being an everyday, every which way, ordinary sort of white black man.

But the political blatantism and immigrationism kept coming harder and stronger. But despite this, there was a resounding sound that mainstream-middle of the road white Britain had had enough. Tayo shut his ears and closed his eyes but still tried not to walk on the cracks in the pavement.

Immigrants

"How's the market?" Steve said.

"It's alright, but you know, too many bloody foreigners!" Mark Braithwaite replied. He was a burly, clumsy young man, who seemed to spend his whole life, no matter what the weather, in blue jeans and the same filthy T-shirt.

"How's Suzie, is she al'right?" Steve gave a lecherous smile.

"She's alright," Mark replied, "she keeps me happy."

"Is she still working in that Bank, you ought to watch her!"

"Don't worry about her. If she misbehaves, I'll give her this!" and Mark lifted up his right arm.

"Alright calm down, I haven't called you here to talk about your missis. What do you think we stand for eh?" Steve said. He was a Fascist with prospects.

"Well we're anti immigration in't," Mark said dryly.

"You what?" Steve replied.

"You know we're against immigrants taking our jobs. You know all the foreigners."

"You can't afford to be this naïve," Steve retorted. "You can't afford to be this stupid. Do you think this is about immigration? Look most immigrants are white! You know from Europe, and those ozzies from Australia. Do you think we're against them?"

"Well no?"

"Your damn right! What about all the blacks and Asians born here? They're British. Yeah some would say they're even English. Can they join us?"

"Hell no!!!.... Well I hope not?!"

"Your damn right they can't, because it's not about immigration. That's just to get the votes. It's about the **spirit of our Race**. It's always been about that. Understand that and you will understand that everything else is just a strategy."

"Now I understand. It's so simple really in't."

"Yeah it's like learning the alphabet: A,B, you just don't forget that C comes after."

"No."

"No that's right you never forget."

Buses fathers, frauds and stupid cows

The spirit of Apathy was sitting on the number 63 bus and giggling with his friend called Chaos. They loved playing with each other.

Tayo Akinjo walked on bus 63 and sat down. His head was buried in a book and he tried to engross himself in escapism. But the smell of insane foot stomping hate was filling up the bus and leaking out onto the street.

The bus was ram jam with black and they looked like character actors in a sordid, nasty little play. Except there was no director, producer and everyone had lost the plot long ago. Feminine black boys with chops and chains, rings and puzzles, gold bangles and slender thighs, their 'maarga' bodies heaped over the bus seats and all over the floors. And they fronted, splenitive, rash, brash and weak. Living parallel lives, with masculine black girls, stomachs like beer drinking football hooligans, breasts around their waists and stupid hair, paid for at stupid prices. *(Yaa Asantewa and Nzingha rolled over in their graves and died. Chaos and apathy laughed until they cried.)*

Fola an anorexic little girl, dragged herself to the top deck of the bus and stared through emaciated half fed eyes at Chantelle. "I wish I had a body like that bitch," Fola muttered to her friend, a short fat roly-poly hermaphrodite girl. They looked like two extremes of the same disease, before and after. They should have been named the degeneration of the noble blameless people. Instead they wore the titles of Versace (fake) and Calvin Klein (fake) all over them, like the branding of corporate slaves.

"Yeah," Fola continued, "if I had a body like that I'd do porn!"

"Scene," her rotund friend said, "I know what you mean. Yeah," and she dribbled down her mouth.

"Not that I'd actually do it" and brushed the brown hair (extensions) away from her face, "but at least it would be an option, you know what I mean. And I'd be getting paid in't, in't."

The object of Fola's complement was Chantelle, a stupid girl, who thought she was 'grown'. She was 'chatting,' in a loud voice at the back of the bus.

"My clothes are in fashion though, I look fit," Chantelle said. Her stomach was hanging over her badly fitting jeans. She was fifteen years old but her womb was rotten like a fifty-year old geriatric prostitute. Her thong was sticking out for all to see and every now and then her used tampon popped up.

"Yeah I've got the lick, I've got style. I told my mother," she said, staring at her friend, a strange creature who did not seem to be part of this world at all (and was dying to leave it). "I mean just look. I'm the business. I'm a real bitch!" Her tampon almost burst out. "Yeah I'm a real bitch and I chat like a bitch!"

The strange thing (her friend) who had only just woken up sort of smiled, "Yeah ...you're the business...you should have slapped her in her clart!"

Tayo was listening and almost threw up.

"What! Shut up you fool," Chantelle replied, "slap my mother! She'll kick my arse! It's not like your family you know! My mother's rough! She beat up my dad and tore out his eyeball. One Christmas he'd been out drinking as usual. And my mother smelt perfume on him. She went ballistic!! Even when the

police came they couldn't hold her back. She was just
screamin,' with my dad's eye in her hand. My dad didn't want
to press charges. You know the embarrassment of being beaten
up by a woman. But the police arrested her anyway. I mean
they had seen her with my dad's eye in her hand. She went
prison. But she came out even madder. She swore she was
going to have the other one if she found him! One time she
licked this Jamaican woman in her head. And another time she
busted up this African, and boy did this African stink, you
know a lot of them do! No offence though. Isn't your dad
African?"

"Nah my Granddad."

"Well, she beat this African woman to a pulp. The African was
saying, 'I don't want no trouble, I'm just going shopping, I don't
want no trouble Jamo!"

"My mother said Jamo. What do you mean? I ain't no Jamaican
and beat her some more. It was funny to see blood on all that
African stuff. You know that stuff they wear to church. You
know all them flashy robe things. You know it?"

Chaos was giggling like an idiot, such good jokes.

"Yeah, yeah, yeah."

"Yeah my auntie wears it sometimes when she goes. They're all
Africans in her church. Anyway my mother beat this African
and there was blood everywhere, it was funny though. So
anyway," she continued, "my body just looks buff these days.
Look at my butt it's just whoa." The fat sagged around her hips
and thighs like an old white wrestler. And she smelt foul.

Tayo shook his head again and tried to shut his ears and close his eyes, but all the filth kept infecting his blood, 'so many Negroes so few Africans.'

She wafted the brown hair (wig) away from her face and stared at her (thing) friend with wide-eyed curiosity.

And further down the bus Michelle was yelling at her younger sister, "you don't have a father. You don't need a father. They're a waste of time. It's mothers that push you out. Fathers are 'shite'! Remember you need to love your mother!"

The rather confused little girl replied to her, "but can a mother make a baby on her own? I must have a father!"

"Just shat your mouth!" Michelle replied, "or I'll push your face up against that window and box some sense in ya!!!"

Tayo sat and frowned in the midst of the confusion and thought of standing up to say something but didn't. Somehow his shiny shoes couldn't hold his weight! But the little girl for some reason was looking straight at him. Not at her sister, straight at him! Tayo. But where were his answers! Her small brown face, wide eyed and searching for the solution to life's eternal questions, but all he could do was sit. 'All this time,' Tayo thought staring at her, 'the earth's been moving, but I've been standing still, an entire generation, perhaps two, has been lost.' His soul wept.

Apathy and Chaos laughed like demons.

Michelle pushed up her bra and smiled through the bus window at a ragged youth who was dragging his heels on the street below, ghetto style, with his Calvin Klein pants visibly sticking to his arse and his slacks by his knees.

Michelle giggled and mouthed something incomprehensible.

He played on his ipod, looking up at her and adjusted his
baseball cap. He scratched his head between the puzzles and
stared wide-eyed back.

"Whose that?" the little girl enquired, trying to peer through the
glass of the double decker as it jostled through Elephant and
Castle.

"Shat your mouth." Michelle replied and winked at the raggedy
boy. He winked back, his **blue eyes** like faded drops in an
ocean. He brushed a blonde strand of hair away from his face,
(it had fallen out of it's puzzle.) His name was Dave but people
called him D 'cause it sounded more street.'

"My niggars how you hanging, what's up," he mumbled at a
group of **black youth** ambling down the street with their slacks
so low, you could smell their arses. They wobbled towards him
as best they could.

"What's up bro," the largest and certainly the most stupid one
said, flashing some gold and silver teeth like a metallic light-
show. His name was Troy and he was an idiot.

"Who're you looking at?" Troy asked, totally obscuring the
other three from making any meaningful greeting.

"Yeah it was that bitch Chantelle, she's on that bus, (and he
pointed at the 63) she's got a booty on her," his blue eye's
flashed and his skin looked even whiter than before.

The others nodded and laughed like hyenas, especially Troy.
Everyone was blinded for a moment, but then recovered.

"I'm goin' to pop that bitch real soon," his face greyed and he
perspired on his top lip, like some Detroit gangster wannabee.

"Yeah I tried," Troy interjected, "but she says she don't sex black men. That there all worthless and only after one thing. Her mum says the same thing. They're hardcore. I got to first base with her and she suddenly started screaming at me and everythin', her mother came in through the door and started punching and kicking me! It hurt like dirt, but I was on it like sonic! I was out of there. She apologised after, but she's not all there, I'm telling you! She said she always freaks out like that if any black man touches her."

"Well that's all right," D said righteously, "cause I ain't black!"

There was silence for a moment, because it was undoubtedly true - D wasn't black!

"Yeah true," Troy finally piped up and almost had an intelligent thought but it disappeared as he looked at his new trainers.

Meanwhile the Number 63 bus trundled through the back streets, because the High Road had been closed, (building works).

Prospects or stupid black woman I

Dionne got on the 63 bus. She had hair, an Oxford degree, stupid ruby red lipstick, £1,000 shoes and she had prospects. Business and finance were her disciplines and corporate finance her aim. With long hair like her saviour and long legs like her heroine. She dreamed of the Black female corporate heaven: where forty-two blue-eyed bachelors dwell, with flowers, chocolates and tickets, to all the best west-end premiers. She had candle lit dinners with her boss John and business trips to Paris. She was climbing the corporate ladder, one rung at a time - of course she was still at the bottom, but she had a lot to learn: as she laid on her back, laid on her front and rolled over, metaphorically that is. 'I work bloody hard,' she would say and she did.

She had smart, sophisticated and sexy written all over her. Literally, every weekend, she had smart, sophisticated and sexy written all over her, her tank top, her jeans, her backside. It was like she needed constant reminding. Of course when Monday started, she was back corporate but weekends, 'one needs to let one's hair down' and she did, right down to her backside. Only it wasn't her hair - she'd bought it. It was from the shop, 100% plastic. She'd given up Chinese! Not the food! Chinese hair! It used to make her head itch.

'Men always think that women have shagged their way to the top,' she thought, 'there was only that one time with John, we were both drunk and we talked about it after. But I would never allow that to ruin a beautiful working relationship.'

Her shit didn't stink, but her breath and her soul did. Her nails black, like the dark tombstones of an imaginary world. All black, 'not a political statement though, God forbid, I've got Asian and white friends!' (but no black ones though!) she always said.

She stepped on the 63 bus and her heels were so high she could kiss the sky, but her feet didn't touch the ground. She had 120 pairs of shoes and was £6,000 in debt, but couldn't see the link. And she always got credit and more credit. Perhaps it was her sexy smile, or her sophisticated walk or her smart repertoire. After all everyone knew she had prospects. She was going places.

She stepped on the bus and scowled at the assortment of low class ethnics that she saw around, *Chaos* and *Apathy* smiled back. She looked at her own skin and wished she was lighter and her hair straighter. She scowled. She scowled at a boy with his trousers round his knees trying to behave like a gangster, and who looked completely insane. She scowled at Tyronne Thomas, an athletic shallow looking young man, who seemed to have abnormally large thighs and a very small head. His car was in the garage for repairs. She sat opposite him and stared at him unblinking. They were like two sides of the same tarnished coin.

Dionne kissed her teeth, "black bastard," she muttered under her breath, staring at him. She had so much hate and it wouldn't turn to love.

"What did you say?!" Tyronne replied. Tyronne's mother had always taught him to respect himself. He was playing football. He was going places fast, especially when he was in his new BMW. He was going so fast most of the time, that he didn't have time to think. His mother brought him up well. Spoiling him within an inch of his life and dragging him to every youth football team in the city. Indeed he excelled there. His mother swore, "when that bastard Aaron Douglass left me I was six months pregnant, I promised I would make the best of my life. No bastard is going to stop me and my family from being a

success," self hate dripped from her mouth like saliva.
"Yeah, you're not going to grow up like that bastard your father
Aaron Douglass are you?" His mother said, almost like it was
an original statement. "You're going to have prospects aren't
you?"

And now Tyronne Thomas, (he'd kept his mother's name) sat
opposite Dionne Douglass on the number 63 Bus.

"You ugly bitch," Tyronne replied, staring back at her.

"You nigger!" Dionne said and she said it like a middle class
white intellectual racist. It kind of stung the air and somewhere
far off something beautiful died: a well, which had been
supplying water for a thousand people in the south of Sudan, in
the Nuba mountains suddenly went dry. Dionne stared at him.
Tyronne was confounded like the lights should have gone on
but they were still off. Dionne abashed - but not repentant,
stood up and flounced off. The passengers on the bus looked
for a while and then one by one lost interest, some flapped their
newspapers or flicked on their ipods, staring out of the window
bemused or picking their finger nails with extreme apathy.

And Dionne Douglass loved her family. Well her mother and
her aunts. There were no black men in Dionne's family! She
saw her mother once every three weeks and went to church
with her auntie once a Sunday. Dionne had a womb full of
sperm but no babies. A heart full of ideas but empty. And she
begged, not on the street and not for money, but in her heart for
love, acceptance and inner peace.

She swung her hair from side to side, swishing and switching,
gathering up speed and spinning around. All that plastic, matted
with dying black hair. And she walked, almost slapping an old
African man with it and then scowled at him, without

apologising, as she swore he tried to look at her breasts. "But I told that black bastard," she thought, stepping to the other end of the bus and looking back at Tyronne Thomas, 'Yeah I told him. Who does he think he is talking to me like that, my father?' *(No you stupid cow, he's your brother!)*

Dionne's father

Dionne Douglass's mother Tricia was married to Aaron
Douglass, a notorious womaniser, one of the original Windrush
generation. But Dionne's mum was the salt of the earth. Even
though her husband Aaron Douglass had three mixed parentage
children and four others from other women, she still stuck by
him. And somehow in the early days, he managed to balance
his competing priorities.

Aaron had never been a patient man, or even smart enough to
look through the deeds of men. He saw the surface of the lake
but not the monster that lurked beneath.

They would egg him on as he played the part of a work
philandering fool. At the bus depot where he worked there were
no secrets. He had worked there for twenty years, but he still
hadn't figured out the boundaries. He prized himself on his
conquests. And thought, 'I can have any woman I want.' It was
like his calling card.

She came!

Short skirt. Even for 1976. Almost nothing top. No bra. Long
hair. It was still the hippy **rage**. She was only seventeen, but
she had the worldly knowledge of a much older woman and
fulfilled the kind of fantasy which multiculturalism always
promised. She was a flaxen haired blonde, with the bluest of
eyes and the milkiest white complexion. 'She is so beautiful,'
Aaron thought, as she skipped into the depot for the first time.
His mouth actually dribbled and it ran down his bottom lip.

"My God." He said to his best friend Derek, who had known
him from the early days in Morant Bay (Jamaica). "I'd like to
get with her."

"You're crazy, that's the Controller's niece!"

"Even better."

"Aaron you're out of your tiny mind! You'll be black listed. Think about it."

"Friend, I've been blacklisted since I was born, look!" and he pointed to the colour of his arm, "Look, I don't check for no rules! If I want her - I'll have her."

Derek shook his head and shuffled his feet. Aaron pulled out a cigarette and smoked it like a teenage film star, but this was no film and he was forty-nine. He took a few long drags and finally, half finished, he pulled it out of his mouth and squashed it. Like a dandy he tucked his shirt in and straightened his tie, walked across the bus yard to the controller's office. She was waiting outside and smiled, pretending to be surprised.

"Where's the boss? Kept you waiting has he?" Aaron Douglass said, looking at her breasts.

"Yes he often does that," she said, looking at his penis.

"Don't worry you can keep me company until he comes. So what you waiting for?" she said, "when you going to take me out?" Her blue eyes glinted.

Right there he fell in lust, but he would have sworn it was love.

"Girl you're fast," he said, trying to look cool and failing, the sweat broke out on his top lip and his hands went all clammy.

"Listen it's not like I haven't been with a man. I know what **you guys** want. I'm open minded," she said.

"Well."

"Listen I've got a flat in Chelsea, just off the King's Road. Sunday 2pm that means we'll have the whole afternoon."

"All right..... Give me the address again," Aaron Douglass said.

"You got a pen."

Aaron fiddled in his top pocket and pulled out a worn out biro.

"Got any paper?" she said.

"No"

"Give me your arm then."

He stuck out his arm and she brushed her breasts against his hands, accidentally on purpose.

"Sorry, I'm just so clumsy. You don't mind do you?"

He shook his head and she scribbled, the pen scratched the skin and drew blood, but Aaron was smiling like a fool.

"See you later," she said, "I'll come back later for him (referring to her uncle)."

Later that week on Sunday

Aaron Douglass made his excuses. His wife spent all day in church with her sister anyway.

He **bounced** down fashion conscious Chelsea like James Dean, Jimi Hendrix and a clown, all rolled into one. 'Number twenty five, Prospects Street, just off Kings Avenue,' he thought, 'and just like them I've got real prospects,' and he looked at how wide his flairs were.

The wind picked up and the clouds turned grey.

The streets were alive with flower power and trendies, long hair and Mary Quant jackets with chic coats. But the only Afro on the entire scene was his.

Finally, he stood knocking. Number twenty-five.

"And it's two o'clock." He muttered under his breath.

There was a pause and a silence.

Eventually, the latch clicked open. The door swung to and Daisy stood there. Naked. Her milky skin stained white: pale, pink, blue and yellow. She wafted the hair away from her face and stuck her breasts out, like a bimbo.

"Come in."

Aaron tried not to look surprised. 'My God,' he thought, 'I've got to try and be cool.' But he felt very black, very old and very confused!

"Want some grass?" she said.

"No I'm okay."

"Let's screw then." Daisy said, closing the front door and undoing his zip.

Six hours later. She still wanted more and like a slave he delivered, until his heart was pounding in his chest and his and her sweat clung to him like stink on doo doo.

At last he staggered out, the rain was pelting down against the window **pains**, and the sky was full of malcontent, he hailed and failed to get a taxi back, she had given him money, thirty pounds - just for the fare of course!

He went back regularly - not to his wife, but her! Every week she demanded more and every week he delivered.

Tricia Douglass his wife wondered. 'What's this new occupation taking up all his time?' but she had church every Sunday and work five days a week.

But once every three weeks, Tricia had sex with her husband Aaron, on a Friday night at 9pm, for precisely ten minutes! She was a good Christian, she let him pull up her nightie, but she never took it off. 'It's a sin to be naked, **except before God**. The Bible is quite clear about that, look at Adam and Eve.'

Somehow, despite all his other activities, Aaron managed to keep this one appointment. 'After all,' he thought, 'our house is in both our names and I've got to keep her happy.'

Then Tricia noticed an itching, a pain in her abdomen and finally a discharge. She was a nurse by profession so she knew what the signs meant.

"Mrs Douglass," Doctor Ramad said (he was her doctor), "you've get pelvic inflammatory disorder and clithomdedia."

Tricia looked at the floor shocked and embarrassed.

"Also you're pregnant."

"What?"

"Yes that's right!"

"My God!"

"Listen I've booked you into a clinic. You've got to get treated straight away, not only for yourself, but also for the sake of the child. The disease has done damage! We'll have to give you a caesarean. Also there is a risk the child may be born with certain disabilities. But I'm afraid there is also a chance."

"What?"

"Your pelvic floor may have been weakened too much, an abortion may have to be the only option. We just don't know yet, until we've done the tests."

"Whatever happens doctor, I'm a Christian. There'll be no abortion!"

She went home and cried for a week and bled for a month. Pain, sorrow and broken promises. Between the operations, she consoled herself with the church but the physical physiological pain was sometimes too great. The book of Leviticus, Revelations, the love of Jesus, beautiful perfect Jesus, blonde and beautiful. His beauty kept her alive. She separated her soul and gave the better half to her saviour.

The baby was born. The mother screamed and the child screamed some more. A badly carried out hysterectomy followed. More bloody and more painful, if that's possible, than any of the blood and any of the pain that had preceded it. But the goodness of the good book consoled her. Though her blood flowed and they ripped out her insides and left them to rot on a metal tray.

Mr Douglass. Where was he?

He'd moved in with his lover. He never did believe his wife's reports. "If you've got something, you must have caught it yourself," he said to her, "don't look at me." The disease and sex flowed between Daisy and him in equal measure.

He played truant from his job: A week off here, a week off there! Why work when you can be a dandy instead! All the best clubs and all the best threads! He was the talk of the town. A poser. A dedicated slave of fashion!

The disease was fermenting and festering in his loins. He grew sick, she grew sick. But it was a sickness that neither was mature enough to acknowledge. At last one weekend. After a week of drinking and drugs they collapsed in a hazy heap. Body on top of body. Daisy woke in the morning in a pool of blood! She was soaked in blood!

The ambulance came remarkably slowly and whisked her away, no questions were answered and none were asked. Douglass sat on the floor alone and wept like a baby. It was the end of his fantasy ride. He got dressed and wiped the sweat stained blood from his face. Reality was knocking at his door.

Yes reality was really knocking at the door!

Aaron Douglass went to answer it.

Three men stood there staring at him.

"Are you Mr Douglass, Aaron Douglass?" the smallest, thickest set one said scowling like a huge wolf.

"Yeah," Aaron Douglass said, wiping the tears from his face. He looked a mess and his relaxed hair was stuck to his head in bits like a buffoon.

"What do you look like?" The tallest one snarled and spat on the pavement.

"What do you want. How'd you know I was.. .here?" Douglass mumbled.

But he, Douglass, had already lost two teeth! Simon (one of the three men) had knocked them out! Douglass sat down on his arse and reached out a hand to steady himself. He had fallen inside Daisy's hallway. Jake, (the short one) who didn't like blacks anyway, stamped on it. And spat on his face.

Blood dribbled down Douglass' cheek and congealed on his chin.

"What.." he mumbled, "I can't understand a word you say," Jake spat, kicking him in his head and dragging him into Daisy's front room. The rest followed.

Douglass' head rocked back and forth as he felt the world whirling, a glass full of wine was smashed across the floor and the room was a wash of red.

"You look a right mess," Jake said.

"Why," Aaron Douglass mumbled.

"Why? Why what! Oh you mean this?" Jake said, "There doesn't have to be a why Douglass. It's about power. I mean I don't know where you guys get off. Who would have thought that a fine English rose like Daisy, would ever go out with something like you!"

Simon, the tallest one stamped on Douglass' head and picked up an antique white Georgian chair, and broke it on his back.

"I mean how is the coon to know," Jake said, staring at Simon, "that his erst while employer Michael or aka Mad Mike Mclean, is one of the most up and coming villains in South London. Don't touch the boss's family!"

"Yeah, you stupid wog!" Pat (one of the three) snarled, stamping on Douglass' testicles, "careful who you're screwing, you dumb black bastard!"

Douglass writhed in agony, clutching his groin. "Please," he mumbled, "I don't want to.. di....e.!"

"Die. You're not going to die. But you're going to wish you were dead," Jake replied, calmly stamping on Douglass' head and partially shutting his eye as it swelled with blood.

"Don't get any of his blood on you," Simon interjected, looking for a weapon to break Douglass' arms with, "He's diseased!"

"Yeah. I almost forgot," Jake replied, "you're right! Find some tools." They scurried about the room, turning over tables and chairs, almost forgetting about Douglass laying bleeding on Daisy's floor.

Douglass coughed, as blood gushed from open wounds. He turned over onto his side, almost falling into the coffee table. He stretched out his hand and felt the glass beneath his fingers. The glass of the broken cup.

Jake stepped closer to Douglass, brandishing a broken chair leg, "I'm goin' to put this across your spine. You're never goin' to walk or touch a white woman again."

Douglass mumbled.

"What," Jake said coming closer.

Douglass mumbled again.

"I can't hear you, talk English will you!" He put his head close
to Douglass' face mocking him.

Douglass clutched the broken glass in his right hand and thrust
part of it into Jake's crutch. The glass stuck into Jake's loins,
blood running down his legs and he screamed in agony.
Douglass scrambled on to him and stuck the rest of the glass
into Jake's face, catching both eyes.

"You'll never touch one either!!" Douglass yelled, spitting out a
tooth. Jake writhed in pain, blood soaking his face and running
down his legs.

Simon and Pat pulled Jake out, even as he thrashed about blind
with rage. Simon was struck dumb with shock but Pat wasn't.

Douglass lay there alone, perhaps for an hour, perhaps two,
unable to move, exhausted, beaten and covered in blood.

Then, the front door creaked open.

Pat stepped back through the shadow. He was alone.

"You know that I'm goin' to really hurt you, don't you," Pat
said, bouncing up to Douglass, as he lay helplessly sprawled in
sweat and blood.

Pat stood over him and his eyes narrowed like a feline predator.

The evening drew onto night, the night onto morning and the
stench of pain, blood sweat and tears, rose up from the
sophisticated streets of Chelsea.

A pretty but stupid black bird with a broken wing flew high in the Chelsea sky. It flew into a parked Jaguar XJS and dropped dead onto the road like a stone. A BMW ran over it and didn't even feel the bump, as its bones were crushed under its tyres. It was a tame wild thing but it never had a chance to feel sorry for itself.

Love, Love, Love.......

Tricia Douglass was the best single mother she could possibly be. She brought up her child Dionne clean and with the upmost decorum. What if her husband had run out on her, she wasn't bitter - though she hadn't seen him since her pregnancy! Dionne didn't want for anything. Her mother was a successful nurse. And she worked hard to keep a roof over their heads.

'He never gave me a penny, not even a phone call. What kind of man is that?' Tricia thought, 'he's probably flinging it about like a Tomcat! But I don't hold grudges against men. Well not all men.' "Just make sure, little one," Tricia would say to her daughter, "that you never marry a black man! They are worthless, useless. Find yourself a decent man!"

And indeed Dionne grew up strong, proud, rich and now she sat slumming it on the Number 63 bus. Her boss had sent her to scout the downtown side of South London for areas of financial redevelopment. 'I can understand why it's important, I just don't know why he keeps sending me?' she thought. 'I hate being amongst all this lot,' scowling at a young black youth who was gyrating his head wildly to some crazy-shouting-music.

'Filthy place, filthy people. Absolutely disgusting, horrible! ' And she played with her new hair. She took out a compact and examined her new eyes. The lenses were almost hazel. 'I'm looking good,' she thought, flicking her hair like Kate Moss. 'I'll look even better once I get that nose job,' she thought, pressing her nostrils together. 'I don't know why I've got such a large nose. My mother doesn't have a nose like that. It must be from that bastard.'(That's how she referred to her father.)

She stayed on the bus the whole way to Goodge Street and smiled a little when she arrived in good time. 'At last,' she thought, skipping past three tramps straddled along the pavement, 'respectability! Even the air's better here!' She narrowly missed a puddle of urine decorating a plastic dustbin and didn't notice the irony!

The red and yellow streetlights blared, blurring the sight and sound of everything. She skipped down a side street and towards Tottenham Court Road. She owned one of the larger penthouses and two other flats opposite.

She looked at her watch, 'it's still early, perhaps... I'll get a drink before I go home.'

She walked to the end of the street and crossed towards Oxford Street. She rang the doorbell of what seemed like a closed private house. A rather dowdy looking man with a bow-tie answered. He smartened up his worn out self and adjusted his woollen waistcoat.

"Oh Miss Douglass, we don't expect you on Tuesdays," he said, smiling and looking at her breasts.

"That's okay," she replied, enjoying the attention and slipping off her jacket, giving it to him. He smiled a lecherous smile and adjusted his glasses for a better look. "Go on up Ms Douglass." He added, taking her jacket and smelling her perfume, he was almost beside himself with glee, his pasty face reddened, his eyes narrowed, "there's quite a few here already."

She click clacked up the stairs two at a time, her heels making indentations in the fake woodwork.

She stepped up and saw the bar with discreet light and soft slow music, with the smooth talking bar steward. 'I know why I pay four hundred pounds a month to be a member here,' she thought, looking at the soft leather seats. She walked over to the bar laconically.

A medium sized stocky man with a Prada shirt and sunglasses, stood inspecting the highly polished teak counter. He ran his manicured fingernails along the surface of the counter. Dionne watched him in awe, inspecting every digit of the contours of his manicured hands. She stared at the cuffs of his shirt, the well-ironed sleeves, his slender back and the way that the shirt hung on him straight. She could see his hundred-pound haircut and smell his aftershave, even from where she was standing. She went closer, his smell brought her closer.

She almost brushed past him and felt the quick sensation of electricity pulsate through her entire body. She sighed and then giggled hysterically like a child. She got her composure and sighed again. Drifting away from him and then getting the courage and coming forward.

'Why haven't I seen him before,' she thought, 'perhaps I've never noticed him. Why he's so handsome.' She sashayed within an inch of him and he still didn't blink. She could smell the Bourbon he was drinking and smiled. 'That's a real man's drink,' she thought.

She plucked up the courage, the whole World was spinning in her head, but she overcame her fear.

"Would you like another drink, Bourbon isn't it?" she said.

"That's nice of you," The guy said smiling, his white teeth almost blinding in their intensity. "I've seen you here before," he continued, resting his head on his hand and eyeing her up and down. She blushed and he smiled.

"What are you drinking?" He continued.

"I'll have sex on the beach," she replied, staring at his blue eyes and gushing with emotion.

"I bet you will." He mumbled out of the corner of his mouth. He brushed the brown hair off his face like a film star or a footballer, or perhaps both. "Sure," he added, motioning over a rather sleepy French bartender, "the lady wants sex on a beach and easy with the pineapple."

"How do you know I don't like too much pineapple?"

"You can just tell. You're a straight up kind of girl - am I right?"

"Yeah," she said smiling and flicking her good hair.

"So what's your name then?"

"Dionne," she said. "And don't tell me, you look like a Mark, a Simon or an Andrew, no Stephen, yes, you look like a Steve."

"That's right, you've really got a gift there," Steve said, laconically staring at her, "And now can you tell me what's on my mind?"

"I don't know," she said, "but it's definitely something dirty," she replied, as she felt his eyes running all the way down her plunging cleavage and over her legs, "it's probably my fault, I've been leading you on."

"So you're a prick teaser," Steve said bluntly, "all that sex on the beach stuff." Ironically it arrived just at that moment in a blue tinted glass with a stupid little umbrella.

"No I'm not going to tease you Steve. But I might sex you though."

"Now you're talking my language. Can I finish my drink first?"

"No you can't!"

"Oh I like that, a forceful woman. Come on then, I'd better get my coat then."

They dangled on each other all the way down the stairs and all the way down the street. They dangled with each other all night. The one-night stand lasted a week, until exhausted and covered in each other - they collapsed in a stinking sweaty stupor of sex, and soiled sheets.

She'd phoned in sick to get the time off work.

But it wasn't enough.

She looked at his taught muscular frame and the pale white buttocks splayed out on her sheets. 'I love him,' she thought, 'what a man, but I need more.' She wafted her hair away from her face.

"I need more."

She rolled over and whispered in his ear, "I want you to tie me up."

"You what," Steve replied, sleepily and wiped his groggy eyes.

"Tie me up and slap me around a bit. Will you do it? I just need to feel that sensation. Don't look at me like that?"

"Listen," Steve said, turning over and looking at her black naked body in the half-light of the morning and feeling a slight tinge of revulsion, "I don't have a problem with it but once we get started, I'm not sure that I can stop."

"Don't worry," Dionne replied, looking with deep love into his blue eyes or were they grey, "I trust you."

So they met twice or three times a week. He tied her up and slapped her around. The sex got rougher and the beatings got harder. At first she passed it off at work as she did some kind of martial art, but now she had an almost permanent limp.

Then.

She missed her period.

Vomited all night, went to see the doctor and sat waiting, she had never liked the home pregnancy kits.

"Well," Doctor Ramad said, he had been her family doctor for over forty years, "I think congratulations are in order, you're pregnant!"

Dionne Douglass stared at him.

"Are you sure?"

"I sure am," he replied, brushing the grey hairs from his face and rubbing his glasses. He peered at her and then suddenly changed his mood, "Do you need some advice on family planning?"

"You mean abortion or something. No! No way," Dionne replied, "my mother brought me up a Christian. I couldn't see myself having an abortion Doctor Ramad, I just couldn't."

"All right. You know you're just like your mother."

"What do you mean?" she replied.

"Nothing. What I mean is, I will be here to support you, just like I did your mother."

"What happened to my mother??"

"I'm sorry I shouldn't have mentioned it. It's really not my place to say anything. But I'm here when you need me."

Dionne wept all the way home and wept as she sat in her apartment.

She heard the door open and Steve stood over her and she wept some more.

She stared up at him.

"We're going to have a baby," she said and sought of smiled.

"What do you mean, we? Aren't you on the pill or something?" He growled and spit flew out of his mouth.

"No!" She replied defiantly.

"You're going to have an abortion!!!"

"No I'm not! It's against my religious beliefs!" she replied and batted the tears from her eyes.

"Religion??! What religion is that?"

"I'm a Christian like my mother."

"A Christian!! Listen with all the things we've done, you ain't no Christian! I've done things to you I couldn't even imagine - till you showed me! Besides, I don't want no half-rape, half ape, half-caste child running around. There's enough of your brothers doing that. It serves a purpose I guess. But not my seed!"

"What?" Dionne blurted, startled, "I never heard you talk like this!"

"Talk like what! I'll talk any bloody way I like, you stupid cow," Steve said, standing over her with his hands on his hips and his Prada shirt hanging creased in all the right places. He looked around like he was on the street. But he wasn't. He was in her flat, alone, "listen you're going to have that abortion or else!"

"Or else what!"

"Listen you know, I know how to hurt you. We're going to have that bastard out, one way or another."

"You wouldn't dare touch me. No one puts hand on me. My mother brought me up better!"

"Touch you, you silly cow! I've done every sick thing in the World to you. As for your mother, I bet she's a right slapper like you!"

"Don't talk about my mother like that! Why are you behaving like this?" Dionne's eyes were all watery and her bad leg had started shaking. "I thought we had something good. We shared some real intimate moments."

"Intimate. You stupid silly cow! I always hate it when you coloureds use these long words. You don't know what you're talking about! Listen. Leave the long words for us. We invented them and we're meant to use them. Just keep on grunting your patois! I don't need your consent for anything! This is my country, I do what I like!"

Half an hour later.

Steve wiped the blood from his hands on to his Prada shirt. His face was covered in sweat.

"It was just a joke right?"

No answer.

"It was just a joke to get an extra hard beating. You love it don't ya, you're always up for it. Init??!!"

No answer.

"Come on you love it?!!"

He kicked her lifeless body.

"Shit, I think I've killed her," he mumbled, wiping the sweat from his forehead with a bloody hand. He looked around for the second time that day and saw his bloody fingerprints everywhere.

"Shit. You stupid cow." And scowled at her. She lay in a pool of blood.

He retraced his steps back towards the front door. It was three am on a Wednesday morning. 'Hopefully nobody's about,' he thought and undid the latch of the door, as the blood oozed from his finger nails and dripped onto the floor. He disappeared up the street, leaving a trail of blood as he went. But the midges didn't even bite him.

Mary and Simon

Genetically modified rats, grown fat on genetically modified junk, fried chicken and Mickie Dees jumped up and down to the vibration of an incessant hidden tune: sublime, powerful and seductive. The tune played on, infectious, insidious, like the worst gangsta rap mixed with the most irritating pop drivel. The name of the tune was Chaos and it was being played with complete apathy.

Meanwhile... Tayo Akinjo's employers were having dinner.

Mary played footsie with Simon under the table, "sorry," she said, not meaning it. The blood left his brain and rushed to his cock.

"This reminds me of old times," Simon smiled like a cherub. "How was the Acharri & Anari Gosht."

"Fine," Mary replied, "and your Flambé Chicken Tikka Special."

"It was alright. I'm glad you enjoyed it. You were always a perfect lady."

"How's Diane and the children?"

"Fine. Why the sudden interest?"

"That's not fair," Mary said, ridiculously fanning her hair away from her face. "I've always cared." She looked around at the ornate décor, and the Indian waiters running to and fro from the bars to the tables. There was a slow methodical thud of some ancient Punjabi music and the sweet smell of frankincense. Sikh warriors rode across the walls in paint and Guru Nanark all silver and gold adorned the ceiling.

The place was packed. "This must be one of the only restaurants in the West End specialising in Punjabi food. You pulled a lot of strings to get a table. I do appreciate it."

"They know me. Besides, there are certain privileges that come as a result of us doing well. You tend to mix with a better circle of friends."

She smiled like a child.

"But don't change the subject," he said, adjusting his Gucci tie. "You were saying, how much you cared."

"I never stopped caring. I just don't want to be permanently in a ménage a` trios, I mean how many is it now?"

"That's really not fair! You know I like women. I never pretended that what we had was anything other than what it was. We enjoy each other's company and that's good. Besides, I hear you like the young athletic type."

"They don't matter. They're no substitute for you."

Simon laughed. The blood was still filling up his cock.

"No I mean it! It's you I will always love."

Mary rubbed her eyes. "It's just that lately, I've been dreading going into work."

"You, dreading to come to work? Come on, stop pulling my leg!"

"No I mean it."

"Why?????"

"It's that Tayo!"

"Yes he's doing well, isn't he! This is his third year and he's finished in the top five executives for the entire district. That Fisher account was a big swing for us."

"I know that but sometimes he makes me feel uneasy."

"How do you mean??" Simon said, leaning forward in his chair, adjusting his tie again and looking nervously around.

"Well he makes me feel like I'm under his supervision."

"I don't understand?"

"Well he's got this stand offish nature. He never socialises."

"Perhaps he's not a drinker."

"I know but there's something which I don't trust about him."

"Are you sure? Surely you mean don't like. That's quite different from not trusting."

"Well, I mean I don't trust him!" She said defiantly.

"Well," Simon said, resting his chin on his hand and adjusting his tie again, "this is serious."

"Well I could be exaggerating?"

"No. Mary you're often very astute about these things. You see a lot of things us men don't."

"Perhaps it's just me. Well. I know he comes from a hard background and he's done well for himself. I mean he's got more qualifications than me."

"Does he hold that over you!! Is he arrogant?"

"I didn't say that."

"I mean that's one characteristic that I cannot abide, Arrogance!" And he looked at his manicured nails.

"We could be making a mountain out of a mole hill?"

"Well prevention is better than a cure."

"But whatever cannot be cured must be endured," Mary added, sighing pathetically.

"But there's no reason why we should endure anything! It's not his company! I set it up twenty-five years ago. I'll be damned if he thinks that he can come here and lord it up! But most of all I don't like to see you upset. You're bloody important to this company! I value you. I don't know what I would do without you."

"Oh you'd manage."

"I'll tell you what, let me have a look at him."

"Oh would you Simon, that would be great."

"That's the least that I can do for my best employee. And my best friend."

"Oh Simon you're making me blush."

"Come on let's get the bill. The night is still young."

She smiled like a small girl with her father.

Simon was a bastard. He didn't know his father and even if he did, he would still have been a bastard, white-hearted, stone cold bastard.

Night and Day

One week later and that night...

He was naked to the waist and covered in blood. The blood of his enemies. And he screamed in the darkness. Red was almost silhouetted against the black of the night sky and his naked torso and his huge muscular thighs. "Kill everyone, kill everything white that moves. Take the white women, rape and kill, use them for your pleasure!" He was joined by more blacks, more hideously savage than he was. Bloody and brutal, with cutlasses and axes, machetes and knives, slicing and chopping, full of gore like wild beasts and black, even blacker than blackest night. The whites of their eyes and their blood red lips, hideously savage. They cut and stabbed. The blood of their enemies ran through the streets and collected in pools on the pavements. Still these savages kept coming with superhuman strength. They yelled, their white teeth shining, "Spare no one, rape, kill. Fulfil your lusts on their women!"

In a nearby building Mary was working late as she usually did. Suddenly the lights went out. She looked around in the darkness and thought she could see movement. "Who's there?" she screamed, "I'll call the police. Who's there? You cowards, why don't you show your faces? Can't you see I'm just a defenceless woman! Will no one save me?"

Unseen hands grabbed her, ripping her dress. She stood their naked and screaming, her white skin pale in the darkness.

"You cowards, show yourself!"

In the darkness a sinister laugh echoed around the building.

"I know that laugh."

"That's right," Tayo said, "it's me!"

"You savage," she screamed, naked, alone and vulnerable. Her white skin, whiter in the night. "You filthy black savage!!"

Tayo laughed, "That's right."

Simon woke from his dream covered in sweat. He pulled the covers off his bed. 'That's the seventh dream this week,' he thought, 'one for every day since I spoke to Mary. I've got to do something. And something fast.'

He switched on the light. And stepped out of bed, doing up the top button of his pyjama jacket. He reached for his dressing gown. *Tap, tap, tap* (knocking on the door).

Simon gave a start, thinking, 'perhaps those naked black savages are here to get me, perhaps Tayo the blackest of them all, wants to kill or even rape me?'

"Are you okay dear?" came the familiar voice. Diane his wife.

"Fine, go back to sleep," he replied, wiping his brow with relief and looking at all the power he had. He tried to comfort himself by remembering who he was.

Simon and his wife had separate beds since 2001. The physical aspect of their relationship was dead. He did his duty with her once a month! The rest of the time he had Mary, his permanent mistress, his massage parlour, the local strip joint and a very expensive black prostitute that he visited every other week. The latter was something that he was trying to get rid of. He could handle the fact that she was a dominatrix and was involved in some of the most sordid sex acts known to man or beast and cost him two thousand pounds a month. But what gave him second thoughts were the nightcaps, at first some hash, then heroin and now straight cocaine.

'Anyway,' Simon thought, 'I'm not spending another night like this. I've got to do something about that bastard!' And he wasn't talking about himself.

Simon

Two days later Simon was feeling the plush leather furniture
with his arse. He sipped a cup of his favourite mint tea and was
just contemplating smoking a pack of his favourite, extremely
expensive cigars. He was in his private club. At number 29
Tavistock Square off Soho Square. It was the second most
prestigious private gentleman's club in the country. Despite that
obvious drawback, it still boasted a number of members from
the Order. That much maligned and now famous organisation
that boasted royalty, aristocracy, policemen and ex-army
officers. 'But really the whole thing was entirely
misunderstood, apart from the two hundred pounds I pay every
month for members' privileges, there are little outward benefits,' Simon thought, trying to convince himself.

His mind turned to the matter in hand. He was tired of bad
dreams. All of them with Tayo's grimacing face.

'What are my next steps, what do I do now?' He thought. He
stretched out his legs.

"Careful old boy!" Andrew Somerset said, almost tripping over
Simon's feet.

"Sorry Andrew, I wasn't thinking."

"That's okay old boy, but be careful."

Andrew put more tobacco in his pipe and turned to walk away.

"Hey, Andrew can we talk?"

"Sure," Andrew replied, he had the confident air of a man who
had his roots deep in the centre of the earth and his aspirations
high in the sky.

"How's it going?"

"Not bad."

"Still making loads of money?"

"Really can't say old boy," he said, sitting down next to him and his spirit filled the room.

"And how's the construction industry?"

"It's okay, but there's so much competition now."

"Yeah from who?"

"You know the Chinese. They're buying everything," Andrew said, adjusting his waistcoat and sitting back in his chair, blowing a large smoke ring from his pipe.

"Yeah I heard they've got their act together."

"It's worse than that, you heard about Sheffield Steel? Yeah well you know they've been a British company since the turn of the last century. And now!"

"Yes. I heard. You're from that part of the country?"

"Yes from Lansing in Yorkshire."

"So what are you doing?"

"Well I've had to reduce my costs."

"By doing what exactly?"

Andrew Somerset sighed and played with his moustache,

blowing the biggest smoke ring yet. He tapped his brogues on the Kashmir carpet, "you don't really want to know," he said.

"Well nobody's listening are they? Besides secrets remain here. Nothing goes outside these four walls. That's the rules, you know that. It won't be the first crooked thing done here and you know half our members are police and the other half are judges. But we'd cease to exist if we were too choosy." He stared at Clinton who was behaving like a fool with some dead caviar on a sliver platter.

"They'll let anybody in here now," Andrew muttered.

"So I hear." Simon replied, now scowling at Clinton. "Anyway, how are you reducing your costs? Please go on."

"Well we've had to let some of the workforce go. You know compulsory redundancies and early retirement. But...."

"Well come on old friend, stop wasting time..."

"Immigrants."

"Pardon?"

"I mean immigrants from Eastern Europe. Their salaries are lower. They work harder. They're non unionised and generally hardier than the British."

"You know I thought it was something really serious. Like you killed somebody or something. That's hardly worth a sleepless night."

"But you don't know the half of it. I mean I employ about thirty thousand. But it's still not enough. So we've started recruiting over there."

"So."

"I mean recruiting is a bit of a euphemism," he chuckled to himself conceitedly, "I mean we're smuggling now, fifty at a time. We've got some places to put them and some understanding friends in the council."

"Interesting," he rested his hand on his chin and sat back intrigued.

"And you know what, despite all the bother. It still makes economic sense. Even if we had to get their papers sorted out. I'm literally saving millions of pounds each year."

"And what if they don't work?"

"Don't work? We've got friends. The police, immigration, they'll be back on that boat before their feet touch the ground. And we like to keep in touch with our patriots too. They can be helpful, especially if that lot get ideas of going underground."

"You know what Andrew, if I had your problems, I'd be a happy man. I've got something far more delicate and yet potentially more dangerous. It concerns an employee of mine."

"Really...... Come on a problem shared is a problem halved."

"So."

"Well it's one of my employees."

"What's his name?"

"Tayo"

"Oh! He's Nigerian, Yoruba I would say. They're generally easy to handle. Any lateness or inefficiency?"

"Well he's born here. He's British. He doesn't even have an accent. I don't think he thinks he's Nigerian at all."

"Oh they're a bit harder!.... He probably thinks he's equal. You have to handle that sort carefully. The other ones, you know who've just came from Lagos, they're so easy. I worked with a lot of them before. They're good for making money. It's their history you know. That pedantic officiousness, all they really care about is money. Give them money and they'll sell you their mother. Plus they're Christians. They worship you already, eat out of your hand."

"But this one studied law."

"Oh a right little Martin Luther King! So like I said earlier, any lateness or inefficiency?"

"Not really, he's usually the first in and the last out, he's made a lot of business for us too."

"Does he use the internet?"

"Yes."

"Any inappropriate use of it?"

"No. Not that I know of."

"Alright then, what about women? That type always has women. Any office romances?"

"No actually he keeps himself to himself. He's not flashy at all."

"But he's **proud** though isn't he!" suddenly feeling who Tayo was and realising how to destroy him.

"Yeah he's proud."

"Well play on his pride. And he believes in justice?"

"Yeah, I think he does?"

"Well play on his sense of justice. Play on his code of honour. Screw with his sense of right and wrong. You watch, you'll get him to resign! You won't need to do a thing."

Simon smiled, Andrew smiled.

Michael

There were two Michaels sitting on the bus, each having their
own problems with the spirit of *Chaos* and *Apathy*.

The first was a mad youth, with mad hair and a ridiculous
looking girlfriend listening to mad beats. "I'm a gangsta
chatting like a gangsta on the mike. So don't even try and test
me."

His stupid girlfriend mumbled, "you know what, I couldn't sit
down on the toilet for two weeks you know. I had this mad
bladder infection."

"That's disgusting," the mad youth Michael said, his brown skin
was blotchy and his massive unkempt Afro looked like he
hadn't washed it in a month and he hadn't.

"Yeah I couldn't even sit on the toilet to piss, it hurt like mad,
you've never seen anything like it," she brushed the blonde hair
away from her face and stared lovingly with brown eyes at
Michael, who was waving his head around like he was insane.

"What, what," in tune with the beat, "I'm a gangtsa. that's right,
the baddest dawg on the block. (the chorus) So don't even try
and test me. I'm just going to upset you."

"So you comin' round for some good lovin," she said, picking
the herpes cold sore from her face.

"I might you know," Michael said. Looking around the bus for
somebody black enough to kill, but there was only the other
Michael.

"Com' on darling," the girl said, (breaking into cockney), "you
can't resist my good stuff," (reverting back to patois).

"Alright," Michael said, "Darling, (cockney) I'll see ya alright scene, (patois) and gi ya some wicked bed werk."

Meanwhile.

The second Michael was a bespectacled thirty something, with a dry sense of humour and a little arrogant streak about him. He had read books and books and the smell of that knowledge was leaking out in perspiration all over his skin. He was trying to ride that bus without losing the veneer of academic detachment, but somehow his sweat just kept letting him down.

The stupid girl giggled stupidly and smiled like she was on crack, of course she was and Michael (one) grabbed his crotch like an LA gang banger and they both repeated "So don't even try and test me. I'm just going to upset you."

The second Michael pressed the buzzer and strode confidently off the bus, *leaving Apathy and Chaos on the bus, singing their favourite tune.* He didn't even glance at his namesake, though the latter scowled constantly at him. He didn't look again until he reached the gates of his university. He was half an hour early.

Michael II

Michael (two) rubbed his baldhead and adjusted his glasses. In his youth he had rolled and smoked, fought and bounced his way through life, like an erstwhile dandy roughneck pimpernel.

'Now that life seemed so far away - how have I changed,' he thought. He tried pushing the idea out of his mind, but he knew as he looked at his brand new shoes that it was Tayo. 'Tayo has been the single greatest influence on why I'm alive. I can't deny it. He was my better half. How did we come to lose track?' and he almost kissed his teeth. Then he remembered that he didn't do that anymore.

He walked the few square miles to his university, flashed his badge like a secret agent and stepped into the main hall. He didn't even look, as the institution loomed around him. The stuffy stench of those intellectual old men, building powers of destruction, in those silent, seductive, secret temples of despair, was rising from the vinyl floors. But Michael didn't smell like them - no he smelt like a cool breeze, on a high mountain, somewhere old, forgotten and far away.

Michael climbed the marble stairs and stepped in Lecture Room 9, surveying the scene. And he thought, changing the subject, 'my students have something that I never had. A teacher that actually wants them to do well. Have things moved on? No. A token face in an all white institution, that doesn't mean progress! Ironic that it's my old institution.' He switched the main lights on and examined the scene. It was like a huge amphitheatre but without the gladiators and the screaming Roman horde.

He took out his books: Destruction of Black Civilisation by Chancellor Williams, The West and the Rest of us by Chinwezu and King Leopold's Ghost by Adam Hochschild. He flipped out his laptop, plugging it in and clicked through the screen of notes.

The time was ticking fast and Michael was going through their possible reactions and processes and how to second-guess them. Then he smiled to himself and realised, 'I don't need to second-guess anything. I've just got to be true to myself and the facts speak plainly for themselves.'

They had already started coming in: John first of course, his politics were to the right of Franco and Mussolini, but somehow he had missed his true vocation. He was going to emerge as a credit to his nation (whichever one could pay him) but for now he was happy to be the grey man. John stared at Michael with inquisitive brown eyes and thought, 'this black guy's really odd, and I should have gone to Imperial College.' He smiled (fakely) at Michael and took his seat at the back.

Ama, Malika and Mathew followed, jostling their way through and then more came, until the auditorium was full of staring, frowning, expectant and indignant faces.

"So," Michael said staring back at them intensely. And with no greeting at all. "What were the principal features of the Berlin conference?"

The class looked around dumb. Tony in the back-row picked his nose and wiped it on the back seat.

Malika played with her locks and blew bubbles with her bubble gum.

Mathew was doodling on his book and Ama was daydreaming of her boyfriend.

The only one who was concentrating was Abdul Hasim. He sat pen in hand, waiting expectantly.

"Well," Michael said, rubbing his baldhead and then the scar on his chin.

"Why don't you just tell us?" Malika said, still chewing gum, "obviously you know. Then we can all go home."

Some of the students laughed guiltily.

"There'd be no fun in that," Michael said, they laughed again, this time less guiltily, "besides I'm not here to spoon feed you. You're not a baby are you?"

"No," Malika said, "but we clearly haven't got a clue."

"Well you said it." Michael interjected, "that's surely the point." He turned to face the rest of the class. "It is you who will be sitting these exams in June. Not me! History is not an easy option. You've got to work. If you've been told anything about my classes then you know that I'm no soft touch! And Mr Wilson stop picking your nose please!"

Everyone stopped to look at him. He shrugged his shoulders.

"Listen, this is very important stuff but you're not going to get the answer watching Big Brother and playing Playstation, you're not! You've got to understand this is only the World a hundred years ago. This is recent history. It helped shape the very way we are now."

Michael paused, he remembered another Michael. He almost saw himself in a mirror darkly: puzzles, twists, carrying a knife, blackboots and a bandana. He put the thought out of his mind. But his pastime reflection kept staring back at him. He adjusted his waistcoat and glasses again.

He continued, "the Berlin Conference was literally where the
major European powers split up Africa and divided it between
themselves. And when I say divided, I mean literally. In some
cases they took a ruler and drew a straight line over the whole
continent. Take a look at the map." He pressed his lap top and a
huge map of the world came up behind him. He used an
electronic marker pen to highlight. "Look at Africa, see the
lines marking Egypt, separating it from the Sudan and Libya.
Look at those with Libya and Chad, Algeria and Mali and so
on. I mean look for yourself see!! Now in most countries the
borders between countries are marked by the action of rivers
and mountains, look at the French and German border. These
borders are the result of peoples over centuries forging a nation
that have similar bonds. But the Nations at the Berlin
Conference had a ruler and a pencil, all they were concerned
about was getting more land. They were not interested in the
welfare of African people. But they were interested in efficient
administration, splitting up and destroying Nations like the
Maasai, Ashanti, and Dinka. Or mixing warlike people into a
nation with their sworn enemies. This would make the Nation
unviable but easy to control for them."

"It's like America taking England and half of France and calling
it the American colony of Anglo-France. And then taking the
other half of France and amalgamating it with Germany and
calling that the American Franco Germanic colony. Then sixty
years later walking away and saying, 'sort it out there's a good
chap, you've got your independence.' How are they going to
sort that big mess out! Only with war and ethnic cleasing perhaps lasting centuries, remember England had a war with
France for over a hundred years. A hundred years war over
boundaries and bloodlines and they call Africa tribal. So with
that kind of historical precedent, how is Africa going to sort out
the issue of nationhood? What does history teach us?"

Wilson sat at the back motioning, as if he had a gun.

"That's right Mr Wilson with blood and guns. People against people. It would be worse than the First and Second World War put together. More civilians have died since 1945 in inter-ethnic conflict in Africa, than all the allied military casualties of the Second World War. So when you look at Africa you see what the problem is. These European powers never intended that their colonial territories would be viable economic entities. In fact they were constructed precisely not to be."

Ama for one split second stopped thinking about her boyfriend and actually thought about the irony, 'if this is so, why are we so proud to call ourselves: Ghanaian, Nigerian, Jamaican and Sierra Leonean, why, why, why?? ' Then she returned to her favourite occupation, 'I can't wait to get back. His body is so fit,' she thought.

Michael smiled. A spontaneous round of applause broke out, (except for Malika) and he smiled again. But then he frowned, "Remember." And his frown was strong, he rubbed his glasses, "Remember." He continued, "I want your first semester paper in by Friday of next week."

The students groaned.

"Yes that's right. And you can include the Berlin Conference if you like. Remember it's on late Victorian Britain."

Goodbyes

'Do you know Tony's dead.' Ade typed into his computer and sent it electronically to Michael.

Michael sat in his office stunned and confused. He stared at the screen for three minutes. The seconds on the dial of the clock ticked. That annoying Newton's cradle banged incessantly. A magpie smashed its head against the glass window and her blood stained the window-pane red. The air conditioning stopped and a comet destined to destroy the earth hurtled into the planet Jupiter and ended up being her slave, orbiting her once every two years. But the earth was saved.

But Michael didn't notice. He just sat.

'No.' Michael typed, 'how? He used to train everyday.'

'Yes,' Ade wrote, 'it was just some freak thing. He just dropped down dead. He had an enlarged heart or something. It was really strange.'

'How did you find out?'

'I met one of his ex's Susan.'

'Susan,' Michael wrote, 'not from the society. I didn't know she went out with him?'

'Apparently they had been for some time. They just kept it secret. I mean, I always thought she liked Tayo.'

'There's a name I haven't heard for a long time. I wonder how he's doing? Probably starting a revolution somewhere.'

'There was always something strange about him.'

'No Tayo's alright, hard headed and bad tempered, but he's one of the few brothers that you can trust with your life. He'd never sell his soul, even if he tried. He's always going to be righteous. Believe me. We went through things together. Anyway what were you saying about Tony?'

'Yes I met Susan, she was so upset, she said she's leaving the country. It's too bad. I understand what she's saying. This place is no place for a black man!'

'What place is our place Ade?' Michael wrote, leaning back on his chair, 'we don't have power anywhere! Where is he buried?'

"It's a massive grave yard, Kensal Green cemetery.'

'That's the place where Mary Seacole is and where Marcus Garvey used to be.'

'Marcus who.' Ade wrote and scratched his head.

'I shan't bother to dignify that with an answer. I'm going to visit him. Can you take me there?'

'Yeah I'm free. Tuesday lunch time,' Ade typed back.

The Grave

Michael stood alone. Ade had sent a text and cancelled at the last moment. Michael used his own skills of investigation to locate the cemetery but now??

Now he stood at Tony's grave and wept like a child. The tears rolled down his cheeks and soaked his shirt. He cried until there were no more tears left and then he cried some more. His brain ached. Finally, his soul was empty and he could cry no more.

He lay a blue orchid on the grave, 'Born, Tony Davis, 12th of 7 1968. Died 1994, aged 26, a warrior, a friend and a man.' The simple inscription read. Michael pulled out some of the weeds that had grown up around the edge. 'He died,' Michael thought, 'eleven years ago and I'm just coming now? How many more are gone? Did we ever really care about anyone at all?'

Michael did up the button of his jacket and stared blankly around. 'The line between life and death is a thin shadow,' Michael thought. 'The permanent infallibility of this life is but an illusion, our attachment to it a joke. Our lives without meaning are worthless. Life is more than the grunt of material pleasures, cars, houses, money, sex, all grunting like a beast. Life is a prayer. A song sung in the moonlight. Live each breath as if it was your last. Walk each step, as if you will never walk again. Speak each word as if it was your last, do your work as if you will never work again. Experience each second and run its course as if you had no more minutes to run. Savour the light of the sun and bath in the glory of the moon, as if you were seeing them for the very first time. Feel the wind on your face like the breath of God. And feel the rain on your face like the waters from heaven. Live and be.'

Michael turned and walked and a rainbow speckled itself across the sky like a Kandinsky painting. Michael rubbed his head as the rain fell anointing his bare skull. And the earth blessed him as he walked.

"I must get hold of Tayo," he said out loud, "this week I must get hold of Tayo and Flex too."

Paradise

Susan looked out at her fields of Amenta, stretching green and brown to the heavens. Everything up to the horizon was hers. Everything beyond the horizon for fifteen miles was hers. Everything right up to the armed guards and the Alsatian dogs that patrolled the walkways was hers. She smiled, as the African sun shone down on her locks, now greying in the evening air. The sun was blood red across the sky, the earth black against the sunset. The heat was thick and the sweat dripped from the encircling trees. She looked out at the lines of cacao plants lined up, end to end, line to line, feeding the ravenous earth with a green leaf here and green leaf there. But the sun was still dying and the moon was chasing her brother across the sky.

She could smell the green leaf and the morning rain rising from the inner firmament of the encircling skies. A bird flew free over the sky and called to a far away nest. Susan looked up and watched as it circled high above, almost lost in cloud and sky, high on the winds of the World. Looking down at the roundness and smallness of the World. And the bird saw Susan standing on her white veranda, with the white picket fences, outhouses and the massive plantation stretched around. The bird saw the fields of cacao and cassava, corn and banana, a patchwork across the Earth. It flew high, too high and lost itself in the swirling patchwork mess of it all and it fell! It fell, like a stone or a creature that had never known how to fly and it fell dead! It never had a chance to suffer sorrow for itself. It was dead and it struck Susan's veranda, right before her feet.

Susan looked down at the black bird lying dead at her feet, even as the sun was dying across the hills. But all Susan could do was stare at this dead black bird at her feet and its blood staining her white veranda red.

"That is so odd," Susan said.

She thought of calling someone to remove the corpse from her porch and she turned to call her house servant.

There was a squawk, not like the sound of anything that she had ever heard in this World, a discordant painful scream, of something old dying. She turned on her heels and looked down. The bird stared back at her, its beak open and Susan froze on the spot.

Andrew and Steve

"Do you want some coffee Stephen?" Andrew Somerset said, unbuttoning his waistcoat and winking at the blonde waitress, who smiled back, "do you like her?" There was a faint smell of Cognac, Whisky and arbitrary power.

"No thanks and (looking at her) not really my type," Steve replied. He winced whenever he saw white women. Ironic. (Of course he would do his duty at some point with an English Rose. But he would never enjoy it. His pleasure was Alek Wek, Dji Dieng, Serena Williams, Aicha, Tyra Banks, Gabrielle Union. Perhaps it was something to do with his mother. In some kind of Freudian reality, she represented working class, aspiring middle class suburbia. She was a rapacious, salacious, obese Daily Mail reader, who ate cucumber sandwiches and prawn cocktail crisps. She was smelly and dull and her husband, Steve's dad, hated her almost as much as his son did. He hated her and she knew it, because she hated him. It was their hate that kept them together. But it was a hate that dare not speak its name. They never vocalised it. It was reserved for the ethnics! It didn't matter which type. 'So long as you looked foreign, you were.') Hate then was Steve's middle name and he was always proud of his pedigree, even as he sat now in the most prestigious restaurant in Knightsbridge.

"So I hear?" Andrew Somerset continued, looking at him and thinking how common he was, "I heard about that issue. You've got to be really careful whom you deflower."

"Listen it's no issue at all, it's nothing," Steve said, adjusting his collar.

"All right. But you came close before remember."

"Yeah and we'll come even closer soon."

"But how's it actually going?"

"It's okay, we did well."

"So I hear. But there is a bigger picture."

"I know. I keep telling them."

"Well. Remember, I have the upmost faith in you. Just keep out of trouble and we will win their hearts and minds. Let's keep in touch. Hey miss, just put that on my account." Andrew said, smiling and doing up his bow-tie. His collar was so white and clean that he could feel the starch on his skin. He grinned, exercising his new dentures and looking at his Chopard watch.

"What kind of watch is that?" Steve said looking at it.

"Oh Just something I picked up."

"I don't know how much that thing on your arm costs?" Steve replied, looking at his watch, "but I can tell you (looking at his Trident watch) this cost me over a thousand pound!"

"Really, that much?!" Andrew said. And he straightened his bow-tie and raised one eyebrow like Errol Flynn. He had already made up his mind.

Flex

Flex was alive. He had a panache for justifying the unjustifiable. He congratulated himself everyday for being an independent thinker. He had never worked an honest day in his life. 'Nah I ain't never goin' work for the system ever.' He looked out of the window at his courtyard. The wide angled brickwork and the stone masonry was magnificent even from this distance. The wrought iron gates cast flitting, flirting, shadows over the courtyard. An oak tree stark and bold had shed leaves everywhere. Flex looked at the encircling courtyard, the paintwork was flaky. 'I need to get John working on that,' he thought, and closed his curtains. He stepped back and walked to the centre of his main hall. The light was filtering through the curtains and sending shadows hither and thither like one big light show.

"God I've made it," he said out loud like a king on a very big hill, "I've really friggin' made it!"

The Black Robin Hood

Colin sat on a pile of boxes in his one bedroom flat. No carpet
or sofa burdened the room and he lit a spliff. The grey windows
stained with filth blurred his vision and the cockroaches
incessant march kept him awake at night. But Colin was as
happy as a pig could be in his own filth. The wooden floor-
boards were stained from constant use and here and there, a
floorboard was upturned to reveal the darkness beneath. Colin
sat up and spat on the floor, rubbing his spit into the wooden
flooring with his dirty foot. Standing, he walked to the kitchen
and turned the tap on, it shuddered and he waited for the water
to turn clear, it never did and he took a chance, putting his
mouth round the tap, he drank deeply and swallowed. He
looked up at his walls and squashed the biggest cockroach he'd
ever seen, 'I'm glad something's getting fat here,' he murmured.
'Cause I ain't.'

His thoughts were broken by next door.

"Will you shut up all that banging? We're trying to get some
sleep. Some of us do work round here!!" they shouted.

"Shut up, shat up," Colin shouted back, his mouth pressed
against the wall like a mad man, "Or I'll come round there and
chop you in ya fo-fo head!"

There was a silence and a pause, followed by more silence.

'Fool,' Colin thought, 'there's no peace for me.'

He looked at his watch. 'It's late!! I got to get there by one,' he
thought.

He dragged a jacket on and pulled a pair of rotten trainers over

his rotten feet, 'I'll get a lift from that cabbie down the road,' he
concluded.

The pissing woman

Del's uncle had run 'Morgan's cabbies since the seventies.' It was the one and only black owned business for five square miles. In the past drug dealers and pimps had plied their trade there, but now it was too rough for them.

Morgan ran the place with an iron fist. During the day, two black Dalmatians (like Anubis) barred the iron gates. It didn't matter that they wouldn't hurt a fly. They were there for effect. The total effect would have put fear into the dead. Iron grates everywhere and an enormous iron door!!! An intercom that sounded like it was in an airport terminal and the slight smell of urine, disinfectant and blood.

Morgan stood six feet three, just like his nephew and with the same attitude. He ran his business on a strictly independent basis. 'I pay no protection to nobody. Never, ever, ever.' He could be heard to say and my, what a collection of weapons he maintained, apart from the sawn off shotgun behind the counter and the pistol in his coat pocket, he had an array of the most exotic and lethal weapons in South London. He cleaned them every night while he sharpened his wit. He could cuss the shine off a two-penny piece at midnight in the full of the moon. He was ready for any scenario, no matter what, where and how.

A youth would come in, trousers hanging down and mumble, "how much is a cab?"

Morgan would peer out from behind the grate, "Wha..."

The youth would stop, assess. But still the ghetto upstart mentality was there. His self-hate was still getting the better of his reason.

"Peckham," the youth would say boldly, "So what you're saying!?" like he was looking for a fight.

The dogs would bark, there would be a rumble behind the counter, like a huge earthquake was starting in the middle of Deptford.

Then the secret weapon: Hortence.. Morgan kept her behind the counter to do the paper work and indeed she was the one who answered most of the callers.

Hortence yelled, "Morgan wah, is lickle foo foo boy, me fel to just quoff him and drag his pants down and spank his bottom blue!"

This of course was always too much for them, as they turned on their heels and made a speedy exit, much to the amusement of Morgan and Hortence.

Meetings and other meetings

Colin kicked open his own door and kicked down the stairs two
at a time. He almost kicked a cat that got in his way and it
purred in defiance. Colin kissed his teeth and stumbled a little
and stepped in dog shite. "Wah!" he blurted, wiping it all over
the landing, "when are they going to clear up this place? This
place is mash!"

He stumbled onto the streets and wiped the remains of the
faeces on the pavement. He stank like a dog.

He did up his jacket and bounced along the street, blowing
rings of smoke in the air. He licked his lips, even as the wind
picked up. He did up his jacket (what was left of it) and
bounced towards the cab office. Morgan's cab office, it was just
off Deptford High Road.

"Yo' got a cab. I need a cab. I'm goin' to Elephant. How much?"
Colin shouted through the intercom. The window was
completely covered by the iron shutter. They always pulled it
down after 10pm.

Another smaller shutter opened on the side of the wall and
Hortence screamed out, "You lickle boy, who you talking to,
what, you 'muther' never teach you manners? You wait there till
you learn some." With that she shut it.

Colin looked at the corrugated iron walls and wrought iron
door and realised that he wasn't going anywhere tonight, unless
he rewound and came again in a different style.

He banged on the door. "Sorry sister. It's late (it was 12.45 am)
and I've got to get to Elephant."

The shutter opened again. Hortence peered out and stared. She looked at him and kissed her teeth. "You magre boy, does ya' mother know you look like that!"

Colin bit his lip and almost wetted his blade. But thought and rightly, 'she looks like she would swallow my knife and spit it back at me.'

"Yeah, yeah, whatever," he mumbled.

"Money first," Hortence rumbled, staring at him with the shutter half open..

"What," Colin replied

"Money first! That's £12."

"£12?"

"Take it or leave it."

"Alright."

There was a jolt and a shudder and the large iron-gate swung to, like an immense iron drawbridge. There was a pause. The night air bit shrewdly. A gnat bit Colin on his neck and he squashed it, blood gnat and all ran down his neck.

At last an old black man emerged from the subterranean darkness and behind the iron edifice and he was cackling to himself, like some sinister night watchman in a horror movie. He dragged his feet in the earth, especially his left, which seemed to be hanging on to his body limply. He looked up into Colin's eyes and he had scars all over his face, congealed and greyed with dead skin.

"Where's your car, old man," Colin mumbled.

The old man cackled again like an old dog and took Colin's money. "Follow me, boy," he mumbled, dragging his feet and scuffing his heels, to what seemed a blind alley. But he kept walking. From the side emerged a secret passage!

Colin almost laughed when he thought of the macabre surrealism of it. And he would have done, if he could spell macabre and surreal, which he couldn't!

Like a scarred Anubis, the old man kept going. It was dark and bleak, bleak and black. Colin couldn't even see his own hand, all he could hear was the scraping sound of the old man's feet as they dragged in the earth. That constant scrapping, like an old wheel being dragged backwards.

At last, the old man stopped, "This is it, boy." The old man said, pointing to an old grey ashen jalopy, with a worn out fender and filthy windows. It looked just like its owner.

"It's not much, but it will get you there. You really want to go boy?" the old man continued and stared at him over the top of his glasses. His face seemed to light up in the moonlight, the grey brown blood shot eyes, still harshly penetrating.

"Come on old man, I paid my money!" Colin replied, walking to the car and touching the bonnet it was ice cold.

The old man dragged himself to the front of the car and opened the door. "Get in and mind your head, boy, whilst you have it."

"What," Colin mumbled.

"Nothing," the old man replied, "come on get in."

The old man turned the ignition, and the car jolted and shuddered, the world seemed to turn around and around for a while. 'I can feel the earth spinning, like I'm on a wheel. Like I'm on a wheel and I just can't get off,' Colin thought and planted his feet onto the floor of the car to stabilise himself. The World whirled around him and he felt nausea rising in his stomach.

"What the hell you doing?" Colin said.

"I don't know what you mean boy, we're here!"

"Where?" Colin mumbled, rubbing his head like he had just had a hang over.

"Here!"

Colin looked out at the streets of Elephant and Castle.

"You know that was quick old man. I didn't even notice..."

"I know." The old man interrupted.

"If I give you an extra fifteen will you wait for me here? I've got something to do."

The old man stared at him from his front seat, eyeing him up and down, as if to say, 'if you've got so much money, you stupid boy, why don't you buy some new shoes?' But the money wasn't Colin's. For this job he was getting paid.

"Yes boy, I'll wait."

Colin opened the door and stepped out. The wind picked up and sent a chill to his bones.

He turned back. The old man smiled, a broken teeth crooked kind of smile, hoping that this youth had changed his mind.

"What's your name old man?" Colin said.

"Aaron.... Aaron Douglass," the old man said with a tinge of regret, "and think twice, is my only advice."

"Don't worry about me, Mr Douglass, just be here when I come back, alright."

Colin slammed the door shut and raced across the road, down Camberwell New Road and looked around in the half-light.

The truck was waiting as promised. The moon filtered through the grey night and the even greyer clouds, lighting everything up like a black and white horror film.

Colin walked to the driver's seat and peered in through the window. The keys were in the ignition. Colin clambered in and switched the engine on.

The truck engine turned over and he put his foot on the clutch and pushed the gear into first.

Colin looked out at the courtyard in front and the pretty painted iron gates and drove the truck straight into them. There was a crash and the sound of metal striking metal at high speeds, as the truck swerved a little on impact, brick and stone followed and was scattered in all directions. Colin applied the break. A trail of dirt swirled up from the debris and scattered over the garden. He put his foot on the clutch and turned the gear into reverse, backed his way out and down Newgate Street.

Colin turned a blind alleyway, sat and waited. He switched the ignition off. The truck shuddered and the engine stopped. He stepped out and counted ten. Then quietly walked down the back streets. Aaron Douglass' car was still waiting. Colin opened the door and sat back.

"Mr Douglass please get me out of here," Colin said.

Flexing

Flex returned late. Too late! But early enough to see Colin's rearrangement of his front garden, he cursed every word in the street dictionary, plus some that he made up on the spot, scowled and hissed like a wild cat, striding past the debris and unlocked his front door.

"So his name is Colin." Flex spat, sitting with his phone pressed to his ear and staring at his Persian rugs and being strangely distracted by a small cocktail stain on the edge. "Damn those cleaners, they never do a good job, that's for getting immigrants." (Flex was still on the phone). "You what, not you, chill man, chill!! Listen do you know where the brae lives?" Flex continued "....Alright let's go and wax him."

Flex put the receiver down and laced up his Timberlands. He reached over and rolled himself the biggest spliff this side of South London. It was so phat! The end hung down like a monstrous dildo. He puffed and puffed. The room filled up and he puffed some more, he looked like a deviant shadow of Bob Marley.

He stretched out like a restless cat and smiled, until he caught sight out of his window of his devastated front garden, he tensed again but finally allowed himself to be hypnotised by the drug. He smoked his conscience away and it drifted with the wind.

"I'm goin' to bust his sledge. Just like he busted mine. But mine is going to last permanently, niggers have got to learn," he spat. (When he said the N word, a very tall tree in the centre of the Amazonian rainforest that had stood for five hundred years died.)

The air was bitter cold. The moon was full and smirked in the midnight sky. A bat flew blindly into a wall and fell down dead. It's neck and wing broken. The gnats were biting and there was just a faint smell of life, slowly dying. Maggots were hatching from the guts of a rat, just beneath the shutter of Mr Tasties fish shop. A fox inspected the carcass from afar, stepped gingerly closer and then stalked away in disgust. And Flex bounced down the alley way and through the courtyard past Mr Tasties, saw the fox, stopped and picked up a small stone. He felt the contours of the stone's smooth edges with his fingers and then launched it, spinning, towards the prancing fox. It struck him on his head and he yelped, and disappeared into the bushes.

"Yoooooossh," Flex said, "I've still got the touch!!"

From afar, the fox stared blankly at him and snarled, white teeth glinting in the moonlight, its tail erect and wagging with vexation.

Flex pressed the key pad on his key ring and his BMW bleeped in response. The central locking switched off. He bounced over, (he was ten years out of date) and looked from side to side, (in case anyone noticed) pressing the handle. He leapt in and turned the ignition. The car purred. The engine turned over and the stereo reverberated to 'f... the police (NWA)'. He put his foot down on the clutch and slipped the gear out of neutral. Putting his foot down on the gas and putting the hand break on, the car revved up, alloy wheels and hubs spinning wildly, he eased off the gas and spun forward, over the **payment** and onto the main road, whisked past the red lights and down Acacia road.

He glided from street to street, up and down and round and round, and finally into Atlantic Avenue. He flashed his lights at an oncoming blue GTI. The GTI flashed back.

He led the way and the blue GTI followed. Together they raced the lights, down back street and alley, up and down, until they left Brixton behind. And from southwest to southeast they slipped through the darkened evening, as it turned into the dead of night. Still the stars flickered and the moon shone bright and the drizzle ran down the windowpanes, leaving moisture stains and a dirty puddle in their wake. Once behind the Camden estates they stopped.

Flex bounced out and Pete parked his GTI and pounced out. Pete adjusted his glasses with his huge bulbous hands.

"Alright Flex," Pete said smiling, "so we made good time."

"Yeah," Flex replied, skipping over a rain puddle, which was forming in the darkness of the night, "so you've got the number?"

"Yeah chill, alright!" Pete said adjusting his glasses, "he's taken business from me too remember before he trashed your yard."

Flex frowned, and stared at Pete's huge gnarled hands. At five foot seven, Pete looked like a Clapham version of Mike Tyson.

"We're wasting time," Flex said, "let's go."

Pete eyed him up and down and adjusted his glasses again, taking off his woollen hat and rubbing his baldhead. He hesitated, and stared into Flex's eyes unflinching. He stared at Flex's angular frame and soft hands, the perfectly twisted but brown locks. The soft smooth face and the slight trace of facial hair under the chin. He stared and he stared, finally resting his eyes on Flex's eyes. He was looking for compromise. And despite the almost feminine demeanour and soft baby hands, he could find none.

After what seemed an eon, he shrugged his shoulders and kicked his heels, bouncing down the street like a much smaller lighter man. Flex followed, smiled, reading him like a book.

The streets seemed to echo their footprints in the cooling night. The bounce, pause, bounce, of two predators hunting. The graceful, sublime sadism of Machiavellian ghettoisation.

Down darkened alleys and concrete tower blocks, through courtyard and greystone. The stone concrete spiralling matrix that is and was Camden estate, reaching up, going round, but never seeming to end. They passed the piss in the passageways, a dead rat or two, rubbish everywhere. Until they stood at 35 Camden Way.

"This is it." Pete said.

"After you then." Flex replied.

Pete smiled. "Alright, my pleasure."

Pete took out his hammer and broke the latch and they bounced in. Colin was sitting on the floor in squalid apathy waiting for his pay.

Pete bounced over, kneed him in his head and Colin was so high, he fell like a stone. They dragged his body out and down the stairs. Binding his hands and feet and put him in the boot of Pete's car.

"I know a place," Pete said, "let's go. I've used it many times." And he had.

Pete

Pete had grown up in a 'respectable' Jamaican home. His mother went to church and his father worked with his hands. They never made trouble, nor did they expect any. They came to Britain just in time to miss the Notting Hill riots and avoided all the other subsequent ones, conveniently. They worked hard to keep a roof over little Pete's head and sent him to the local comprehensive in Forest Gate with a clean satchel, white socks and a smiling face, every, single, day! He was the apple of their eye.

He was short for his age and stocky, even at age five and the black boys used to pick on him, calling him an ape. Little Pete grew up bitter and cried almost every night. And his tears turned his blood to ice.

His Dad ever practical - stared at the boy's awarkedness and smiled, thinking of a solution. Then one evening on the 3rd of June 1978, the boy was only ten. He dragged him wide eyed and curious through the back streets of Bethnal Green, in through a side entrance and finally into the dirtiest, smelliest and hardest gym in East London. The boxers were in and the gangsters were there every night looking for potential bouncers. But ten-year-old Pete just stood and stared.

The smell of blood and sweat was intoxicating.

"Get in their boy," his father said, taking off his jacket and helping him remove his track suit bottoms.

An old beaten man, with cauliflower ears, a limp, and what looked like yellow and grey skin stared down at him. The stench of sweat was overpowering. "It's been a long time Beres, when you going to come back?" The old man's eyes almost black within white pools shone with life, though the rest of him seemed to be decaying.

"My time of fighting is over," Pete's father replied, "but this is my son. See what you can do."

And he did.

The old man worked the boy and turned his fat into muscle and his awarkedness to pain. Pain that he inflicted on his opponents. But it wasn't enough. He wrecked the face of every boy in the gym, and trained three days a week. His studies took second place. After all, "this is where you get respect," young Pete would say.

By the age of sixteen he was boxing as an amateur in the adult division. And knocking the men out of the ring one by one, until no one would face him and he got bored.

He was regular in his training: every Wednesday evening, Friday night and Saturday morning.

But this Wednesday he missed a meal, he didn't know why and instead of his half an hour run, he only did fifteen minutes. He was early at the gym by a full hour.

The lights were on.

He had never been this early in six years. He tried the door, and stepped in.

The canvas was wet with pain. Elbows and knees flying and the sound of crunching bone on glove. Clinch and rebound, step around and twist, hip, elbow, block and knee.

"What is this," Pete said almost to himself?

"It's Muay Thai, or Thai Boxing to you," a tall slim angular and rather fierce but controlled looking black man said, stepping out of the shadows and staring at him.

But Pete was just looking in the ring.

"I want it," he said. "I want in, I got to have in." He reached inside his pocket and pulled out a wad of notes and handed it to the tall man. "Whatever it takes I want in."

The man smiled back, sticking the notes in his tracksuit pocket and staring back at the ring, "Whatever you say. But not everyone is a natural fighter. You got to take before you can give."

But Pete wasn't listening.

Pete kicked, elbowed, punched and kneed his way through five more years of Thai boxing championships and the gravy train rolled in and deposited its wealth on his lap.

His club sold their reputation on his name. 'Pete the Punisher.' Local shops wanted him. Come and open our local store in Forest Gate etc. etc.

He was seduced by the fame - for just a little while and it was salacious enough.

Mad Mike Mclean the big bastard of South London sat at the ringside, eating something foul and sweating in his new grey suit, as Pete demolished 'Dangerous Dave from Deptford.' Mike smiled a sought of half smile with broken teeth. "I like that," he grumbled under his chin, "it's al'right. Go on my son, you black bastard, chin him!"

Scouting

Since the Aaron Douglass problem, Mad Mike Mclean realised
that having some blacks on the payroll could yield dividends.
He employed and petted Pete. He gave him chump change,
wads of it and tried not to slap his arse. Pete drove a car with
2BHARD as a number plate. And he manoeuvred through the
streets of South London like a pimp. Silver chops and Gucci
shoes, Prada shirt and three gold teeth.

Pete lifted weights and got henched. Screwed thirty different
women a week like a rock star and smoked pure Cocaine. On
weekends he was for hire. Mad Mike gave him money, and
more money, £5,000 to hurt him badly and £10,000 for
something serious!

Pete rented a flat in Covent Garden and **spat** money on his
latest gadgets. He smoked weed almost every day, drank the
latest champagne and ate the most expensive caviar, though he
didn't even like the taste. By the end of the week he was broke.
Pete was riding high and living the black British dream.

The door came crashing in.

It was three am and the sun was dead.

The door came off it's hinges and broke it's fall on Pete's
favourite dressing room table. There were bits of wood and
metal everywhere and a nail and hinge too.

Pete rolled out of bed, slipped on a dressing gown and scrambled around, trying to gather his thoughts. 'Where's my gun.'
(It was downstairs in the kitchen washing machine, under a pile
of dirty clothes for sake keeping).

He reached for his samurai sword; he kept one for ornamental purposes on the wall but its edge was razor sharp.

He drew the blade and it shone in the darkness of the morning night.

He stood up and stepped gingerly towards his bedroom door.

Turning the latch and the knob, he stepped out of his room and looked down at the landing. He saw the broken door and the smashed table. He realised too late.

A gun butt struck him on his jaw and he stumbled back and he deliberately dropped the blade, he knew the drill.

"Get on your knees you bastard!" A heavily armed and armoured man said, staring down at him. The man pointed a shotgun at his face and three others joined him, one pointing at his groin and another at his heart. A fifth covering the first and sixth was on look out.

"It's the .."

"I know who it is." Pete said, laying on the ground and spitting out a tooth.

"Do you think," The sixth police officer said cuffing him rather too tightly, "that you could get away with all of this?"

Pete smiled and wiped the blood off his remaining teeth with his tongue. And he didn't talk. In fact when they sentenced him to fourteen years in jail for possession and attempt to supply Cocaine, Cannabis, actual bodily harm and grievous bodily harm, with fifteen other offences to be taken into consideration, he still didn't talk. He almost smiled as the Barrister **read** out his crimes. The rap sheet was like an ovation of his life.

Mad Mike never forgot that Pete 'kept stum.' There were still benefits to be had in prison life. Pete knew how to work the system and he slowly eased his way into becoming the 'daddie of his wing.'

Days and months went quickly and the initiation into the fraternity of the professional thief went well. Even after he was released. There was always a need for efficient and clinical violence, without emotion. Pete had buried his emotion deep, in the bottom of his soul. Occasionally he did the odd freelance work. It was always messy, but it earned more money. That's how he found out about Flex. It wasn't hard really. Flex drove around flashing his money about town like a playboy, 'didn't he go to college,' Pete used to think to himself. 'Strange with all that learning, he couldn't find something more intelligent to do: but money is money.'

And now Pete stood with Flex in the middle of a field in Hertfordshire, at two am, staring at Colin, spitting blood.

Colin lay there bound, the blood from his head oozing out.

Flex pounced up close to him.

"Have." Flex stamped on Colin's head. "You," Flex stamped on his jaw and it seemed to crack as the boot struck. "Learnt," he stamped again and a spurt of blood shot up Flex's shoe and splattered on his leg, "your lesson!" And Flex kicked him in the ribs.

"Please." Colin mumbled, stretching out a hand pathetically and clutching onto the grass of mother earth. He writhed on the ground like a wounded deer hit by a car and stared up at Pete and Flex. The blood soaked his eyes and he could feel his brain pounding inside his skull like a locomotive train. His shoulder

was dislocated and he could feel his left arm was broken.
The pain was shooting up and down his body, in spasms. He
was losing consciousness. He blinked the blood out of his eyes.
Even his eyebrows hurt.

"Please," Flex mocked, stamping on Colin's head again. He
laughed. "And look, you made a mess of my jeans, you black
bastard!"

Just then the conscience that Pete had buried - surfaced, strong
and hard and kicked him harder than any man had ever dared.
He remembered all the pain he had inflicted. All the innocent
victims he had put in a box never to see another day. "Man
your cold," Pete said, almost surprised by his own words, and
he shook his head.

"That's right." Flex replied and smiled, a sort of shadow hung
on his forehead like the night sky had marked him. And he
looked Pete up and down.

"You're a God damn hero when your opposition is begging for
mercy. God what a hero!!" Pete said and turned on his heels
like a much lighter man and bounced towards his car.

"Haven't got the stomach then," Flex replied? "You're a light
weight!"

Pete swung round and stared at Flex hard. Flex tried to keep
the stare, he really did. But there was still something cold in
Pete's soul and Flex didn't want to heat it up.

Pete smiled, "if you like," he said, bouncing away. "But I'm
never goin' to work with you again. In fact I've had enough of
this crap. Beating up people who ain't nothing but victims
themselves! I've had enough. I'll see you around. Have a nice
life," but thought, as he bounced away, 'can you feel it when

you're cutting off your own fingers and toes to spite your body and your nose to spite your face. Even when your sitting in your own blood. Do you really notice it', and he jumped in his car.

Flex smiled, "Not so tough after all then," he muttered under his breath, spitting at Colin's lifeless body and trying in vain to wipe his blood off his shoes. Flex watched the moonlight reflecting on the bonnet of Pete's car as it roared away. 'A real light weight.' Flex thought and crouched down to rifle in Colin's pockets. "Not even a fiver," he mumbled, and gave him another kick in his ribs.

'I'm out of here,' he thought and looked around to see if anyone was watching. He jumped in his car, turned the gear into first and put his foot down on the gas. A fox jumped up and hit his headlights.

"What the fuc.."

Flex stopped and stepped outside, almost expecting to see the dead carcass. But there was nothing.

Flex wiped his face, for the first time in his entire life he had started to sweat.... and he sat back in his car. He turned the ignition on and sped away.

Colin's blood was still wet and the earth was drinking it.

Flex finally stepped blankly through his front gate.

He snarled, "what kind of dog, no wait, that ain't dog, more like a....... fox?"

Faeces lined Flex's driveway and front door and the remains of three dead rats, rotting, had been deposited on his porch. The stench was overpowering. It smelt like death.

"That's nasty." Flex grunted. "That's just plain nasty." But the smell of death wouldn't go away.

At the laundry and after

This stain won't come off sir. The rather nasty looking Turkish gentleman (Ferhat) said looking at Flex.

"Look I pay you good money, just get it off," Flex replied, looking at his chops. And eyeing the décor of Ferhat's business.

"But sir?"

"Don't argue, just sort it out alright. I'll give you a week. When it's done, give me a call. Or better still, I want you personally to deliver it."

Ferhat stared at him.

"Is that okay?" Flex asserted, biting his bottom lip.

"Of course sir." Ferhat replied and sweated a little.

A week passed.

The front door bell rang. Flex bounced down the stairs two at a time. "At last my jeans, it's about time."

He turned the latch and flicked the door open.

Expectant and waiting like a child at Christmas, Flex stood on his newly renovated porch. The chrome gate railings shining and the newly cemented porch finished off with white Cheshire granite.

The sun shined, though the wind picked up and sent leaves rustling over the morning sky. 'Today is a good day,' Flex thought.

Ferhat stood sheepishly eyeing the ground like a naughty schoolboy. So there they both stood like children, one gleefully expectant, the other apologetic and shamefaced.

At last Flex got some maturity. "So it's all done right?"

"Not exactly sir," Ferhat replied, trying to wipe the concern off his face and failing.

Flex hastily grabbed the parcel and feverishly tore the plastic off.

"Now sir, we've talked about this, you're one of our best customers and we've never had a case like this before. And we know you recommend us to your colleagues, we've received a lot of business through you.... but...."

There was endless plastic but finally Flex pulled his jeans out and he stared.

"And sir we wouldn't want you to think that we didn't treat this matter seriously. On the contrary..."

Flex stared at the bloodstain. It was now black! Flex shook his head like his soul had been touched. The wind grew stronger and the leaves bustled round them spiralling and funnelling across the porch.

"So we've decided to give you your money back and offer you a month's free service..."

Flex stared at the mark, 'I swear,' he thought, 'I swear that this mark is in the shape of Africa with Madagascar and all, I swear,' and his eyes swelled up with tears.

"So sir.."

"Stop." Flex said, "just get out, go on just go. Keep your money just go. Honestly, don't worry just go."

Ferhat stared at him, nodded and finally trundled off across the porch and through the gate.

Bedside manner

Flex woke up in a cold sweat. He stared blankly at his room, and stepped on his plush carpet. Wetness oozed between his feet. "What's that." He mumbled, out loud and to himself and, "what's that smell?"

He flicked the light on.

There where he had put his jeans on the chair, the carpet was all covered in blood and it had dried black.

"How can this be." Flex mumbled again. He stared at the pattern, 'I swear,' he thought, 'this looks like the shape of.....'

But he pushed the idea out of his mind.

One day later.

"I'm sorry sir," the carpet cleaner said, "the stain won't..."

"I know," Flex said staring at it, "come out!"

"It's strange," the cleaner added, "it looks," he rubbed his chin like an academic and he wasn't. "Just like the shape of Africa. You know I've been to Africa. It's Wonderful. A wonderful continent! The women are out of this world! Shame about all the poverty."

"Really," Flex replied, breaking out in a cold sweat again, "haven't you got something else to do?"

"Oh sorry, I didn't mean to offend you. There won't be a charge of course."

"Of course."

"You should go to Africa sometime, it might do you some good. Aren't you from there? You look like one of those Berbers or Askaries." He looked Flex up and down.

Flex stared at him.

"Sorry mate, so I'll be on my way."

But the tears and the anger had already welled up in Flex's brown eyes.

Good Bedside manner

It had taken a week of bribing and threatening every drug
dealer he had ever known. But finally Flex stood outside the
hospital. Colin's hospital.

He didn't stand on ceremonies and his Timberlands' click
clacked up the shiny stairs and along the shiny corridors. The
smell of disinfectant and death was overpowering. And Flex's
face was wet with sweat, as it was almost every day now. His
locks hung lank on his face, no bounce, no rhythm, no life.

Flex went up to the front desk. "Can you tell me where Colin
Simon's bed is please?" he mumbled.

An overworked and bad tempered Mrs Akinjo stared back. She
should have retired years ago, but she still did weekends and
evenings for the extra money. She looked at Flex's locks and
half felt like saying something rude. 'He's probably a jamo,' she
thought ignorantly and waved him down the ward, "Bed nine
on the Charles Lynch ward," she said.

Flex looked at her for a while like he should know her, the
shape of her face, the eyes, the mouth rounded and perfect, but
his intuition had been failing him for some time, ever since he
had filled his soul with other people's blood. So he just half
bounced away, reading the names and the numbers. The earth
seemed to be rising and falling, undulating, like some huge
roller coaster, 'but who's driving, it ain't me!' Flex thought, 'the
sky is spinning round and round, like a merry go round and
there is that smell of blood.' He couldn't get the smell out of his
soul, 'blood, nothing but blood.'

Flex could feel his breath shortening and the air leaving his
brain. He steadied himself trying to find the strength to breathe.

His chest tightened and perspiration broke out on his back.

He rubbed his hands together, they were clammy and hot and he tried to iron out the furrows in his brow, but he couldn't.

The room started shaking, the air cleared. At last he stood at bed number nine. He sighed and breathed.

There Colin lay: A tube sticking out of his mouth, the ventilating machine's electronic bleep, bleeping.

Flex approached the bed gingerly, and stared. The right side of Colin's face had caved in and there around what was left of his jaw, was the unmistakable sign of Flex's boot mark. Flex winced and frowned. There was no nose or cheekbone, just dents where a face had been, a mass of blue-red scar tissue and stitches.

His body lay lifeless. It was bent double - abnormally twisted.

He went closer. Colin's eyes flickered. For a second Flex thought he opened them, but they were closed - surely! His body seemed to sigh for a while, his chest rising and falling.

Flex stepped back and rubbed his forehead, flicking his locks out of his face, 'these locks are nothing but vanity,' he thought.

The smell of blood wouldn't go, it was rising stronger and bolder, an overpowering stench of dying.

Flex looked at his handy work and a single tear dropped down the side of his cheek, 'this is the first time that I have ever felt genuine emotion for anyone other than myself.'

Flex looked at the starched white sheets and stared, hoping for some movement or gesture, as if this would nullify the pain.

The sheets were so white, but there in the centre of the bed, just above where Colin's heart lay, there was a stain? Flex looked around, 'that's strange, I'm sure that wasn't there before, perhaps it's my imagination.'

But if it was imagination, it was growing stronger.

"Surely," Flex repeated, "that wasn't there!"

And sure enough the stain, which had once been a dot, had grown to a fist in size - blood red. The odour was intoxicatingly pungent.

Flex watched in horror. The Blood was spreading on the sheets and running down the bed onto the floor. And there on the white sheets the unmistakable sign. "I swear that is the shape of Africa," Flex said, openly weeping like a baby. He turned on his heels in terror and ran like a small babbling feckless child, weeping feverishly.

But the blood kept running, though the orderlies came to mop it up, blood and more blood. The stench rose to the high heavens.

Cromwell Road

The barber on Cromwell Road, Deptford, had stood for fifty
years servicing black people's hair, but Flex walked towards
there with extreme trepidation. Half way along he stopped,
paused for breath, his chest tight. He could feel the air leaving
his lungs and he gasped like a spent swimmer.

He steadied himself, waited, leaning up against a nearby
lampost and winced down the road as the morning sun
glimmered through the concrete trees.

A fat woman walked past. She was fat and she wore a wig:
dead, blonde and very long. And she had the kind of fat that
hung on her like it was trying to escape. All her parts were
trying to leave her: her breasts sideways, her butt outwards, her
stomach forwards! But she held it all in with lycra, spandex
and a most ridiculous short skirt!!

Her face was painted with the faint smell of dying womanhood
but the faintness was fading and real death was taking over.
She was kicking three children down the road and wretching at
them like a maniac. One of her boys: six years old, already had
some of his mother's madness and ran up to the lampost Flex
was leaning against and booted it with his Nike trainers.
Kicking it, kicking it, incesantly, with all his might, until he
himself was kicked by his mother, as she ran up behind him.

Flex stared at them, forgetting all about wheezing and
coughing. He steadied himself. The woman scowled at him and
then her frown turned to a smile, as she looked him up and
down (Flex preferred the frown).

"I know you," she said and her teeth were yellow.
Flex stared back.

"I know you," she repeated, "your Flex init!"

Flex kept staring, even as her six year old in his Nikees gawped at his leg and thought about kicking that instead.

"I'm Melanie!"

"What?" Flex said, "not Melanie from College....no?"

"Why have I changed that much?"

Flex smiled.

"I still look good init," she continued, as her makeup ran down her face and stained her spandex.

"Yeah, yeah," Flex blurted feeling sick.

"You always used to fancy me, didn't ya, everyone did, everyone likes me!" she added, even as her children had resorted to throwing stones at the cars going up and down Cromwell Road.

"Yeah... well, you know, that was a long time ago," Flex continued, "aren't you married. Look you've got three children, aren't you married!!?"

"I was married to that one's father," she continued, pointing at the six year old, "but the rest just happened, you know?"

Flex nodded not knowing, because despite all his madness and depravity, he still held repoduction a most sacred act.

"So why don't you come round and visit me. I know you likes me," she said.

Flex had been talking to her all this time and only now had it dawned on him that this was actually the same Melanie from his college, all those years ago. That same Melanie who men fought with fists for. The revelation almost knocked him down. If he had remembered to bring his knife he would have used it to cut his eyeballs out, so he could keep the memory of how she was, unmixed with the reality how she is!

"Do you still keep in contact with that brother, you know Tayo and that other one, what's his name Michael?"

Flex shook his head trying to block their names out of his subconscious.

"Listen, here's my number, have you got a phone?" Melanie said, all the while her children were running madcap across the road, even as the traffic honked their horns at them.

"Are they okay?" Flex asked pointing to them.

"Don't worry about them, it's you I'm interested in," Melanie asserted.

Flex stared at her and saw her transformed into a fearful gargoyle. Her eyes red like fire and her mouth dripping purple tree gum. He could feel her swallowing him up and consuming him, locks and all, so nothing was left, except another one of those fearful children. Her perfume, the honking of the car horns, the screaming children, the dead wig, Mother Africa bleeding, dying. He felt sick.

He vomited, just missing her. The vomit dripped from his mouth and splattered over the pavement. He wiped his lips. "Ugh," Melanie gasped, backing away wide-eyed and shaking her head, "Anyway, I've got to be going, see you around, when you're better," she blubbered and toddled up the road, kicking her children with her.

But the whole World was turning and Flex was in the middle of the merry go round. The old Flex would have gone home and sat in a bath for a week. But the new one knew he would only be sitting in his own blood.

'She,' he thought, 'she, is a reflection of me. It's not her that's the gargoyle or the tyranny of evil men, it's me!!'

'I need to cut this hair off,' he thought and dragged himself away from the lampost, staggering up the road, even though his soul was pounding through his skull.

The barber shop on Cromwell Road was ran by Papa as he liked to be called. He was an old Black Panther, reformed drug dealer, relapsed Black Muslim, in fact he had been everything that it was possible to be. Malcolm, Marcus, Marley, and Martin adorned the walls, with a big picture of George Jackson (with his scarred fists) above the door.

As Flex skipped in, Papa watched him with reserve. Morgan, Del's uncle had taken a break from his cab shop to get his hair cut and he lolloped over to Papa, whispering in his ear. Papa stared at Flex.

"Yes my young brother can I help you!" Papa said and eyed him over the top of his spectacles; he only wore them for affect.

"Yeah old man," Flex said. "Scrape it clean." And he took of his cap and his locks fell to the ground, "scrape it, scrap it and trash it as waste. I'm going for a clean start."

Papa looked at him.

"Nah man, we don't do that here. You're looking for a lesson."
He stared into Flex's eyes. "I don't judge, but I don't like what I
see. Look take this." And he handed him a card.

Morgan frowned at Flex and looked him up and down.

"She deal with ya," Papa said smiling and then frowning.

Flex half thought the old man was joking, but then he looked
again. Nobody was laughing. Everybody had stopped cutting,
smoking, joking, texting, and they were all looking at him.

Flex realised he was out of his manor and he stared at the card.
"Alright, cool, I'll call her."

"That's right," Papa said. "And can you leave my shop now, I
have to clean up the blood?!"

"Blood?" Flex said.

"Yeah!!!" Papa said, fetching a mop and mopping the entrance.

"Alright (disbelieving) I'm gone." He stepped around the wet
floor and shut the door behind him. He looked through the
glass and stared at the shop, the conversations had started
again. He stared through the window at Papa's floor and
swore that he could see a stain of blood where he had walked
in the shape of Africa. He shuddered and walked up the road
putting that thought out of his mind.

Hortence

Had grown up in a convent school in the north of England. She was seven years old in the nineteen forties, when it wasn't fashionable or normal to be black. She was beaten and abused, though her father had fought and died flying aeroplanes in World War Two for England in the Battle of Britain. Hortence his daughter struggled and suffered. Her mother had been committed years ago and after a few years of electric shock treatment, bread, water and pork pies. She couldn't even remember her own name, let alone that of her daughter. She was abandoned. A fact not lost on her school friends as they teased her. They were really the pride of England, the flowers of this sceptred isle. The little devils revelled in Hortence's innocence and vulnerability. They pulled her hair and spat at her, all the while the nuns (her teachers) taught in class that black people were the cursed children of Ham.

She cried herself to sleep every night and asked God, Jesus, Moses, the Virgin Mary and just about anybody else she could think of to rescue her. But they all must have been out that night and each and every night, because nobody came to answer her call.

She cried and part of her soul died. But the greater and better part lived. The tears dried up. The arteries hardened. The blood cooled. But the spirit lived. She got old and left England's shores, travelling the world. She went to Japan studying Reiki and found out she had a panache for healing and that being the only black in town didn't matter to her. She went to China learning Feng Shui and Qi Gong, India for yoga and massage and Haiti to learn Loua. She got on a plane to Benin and learnt Mami Wata and travelled back through Jamaica to study Herbalism and stepped off finally in Brazil and immersed herself in Candomble. It took her thirty-five years! She came

back a master in ten arts, and then rejected them all for the
music of her soul. She played the fool to catch the ignorant, but
there was a spark of divine power that ran along the soles of
her shoes as she glided, yes she glided, not walked. 'Look,' the
boys would say, 'the soles of her feet don't touch the ground.'
But she would just stare at them and cuss. She only smiled
when she was alone and when she knew she could.

The Sister

Flex flicked open the door and looked down his long garden at his metal gates. A small diminutive black woman stood intently waiting. He did up his Gucci dressing gown and his matching Gucci slippers and pressed the switch. The huge gates swung open. She strode in, locks covering her face. Flex peered to see her, but her locks were too thick, the natural grey ends almost reaching her waist. She glided up the garden path in zigzags. Then she stopped. Her black Fubu boots hovered at the edge of the newly mown lawn. She sniffed and caught the faint smell of rhododendrons, "nice smell," she said. There was no trace of any accent whatsoever in her voice, it seemed to come from the ground and gurgled like an underground stream, "yes nice smell, bad house, bad man."

Her head looked up towards Flex's but still he couldn't make her out. 'Her feet don't touch the ground,' Flex thought, but then shook his head convincing himself otherwise.

She rummaged inside her bag and pulled out a glass bottle. It glinted in the morning air. She unscrewed the top and splashed some of the contents over the garden path.

She yelled, "he trashed your garden didn't he?!!"

"You what," Flex replied, startled and he started shaking.

 "I liked what he did," she said and spat on the path.

"You what!!" Flex said again and made a motion to lay hands on her.

"What you going to do?" she replied and Flex became acutely aware of her eyes, two black pearls staring at him.

He stopped.

"Are you going to break my jaw as well?" she said.

"How do you know about that? Who told you, who told you???"

She walked closer to him and her gaze was fixed. They burnt a hole almost to his soul.

She walked closer and stood on his porch. "You're not a devil though, you've just let wickedness grow in your soul."

"Oh you're not a Christian?" Flex said, becoming irritated. "I just phoned you for a hair cut. The old man said you could do it."

"It's not a hair cut you need young man. Like all of our people scattered across this world, we need a wake up call, to wake us from this nightmare," she said, suddenly coming near him. Flex realised though she moved like a young woman, she was very old. He shuddered a little more.

"Are you cold?" She said and stepped right up to him still staring.

"No I'm all right."

"No you're not, there's blood on your hands Flex, look!"

"How do you know my name? I didn't tell you that over the phone." And he raised his hands with the definite intention of throwing her out of his house, off his porch and out of his life. But then he felt the sensation of something warm and wet drip on to his porch. He looked down. There in the crevices of his fingers, between the veins of his hands was blood. The morning sun wasn't very high in the sky, but he could see the red liquid dripping. The smell was overpowering.

"You wait here." Flex replied, agitated, trying to gain composure, "you wait here. I'm going to wash this off. Don't move from here. Do you here!?"

"Yeah, sure," she said.

Flex strode into the bathroom and went straight to the sink, without even turning on the light.

He turned the handle of the hot tap and stuck his hands in the water, feeling the refreshing water oozing out onto his hands. He sighed.

"That won't wash it away. You need something else." Flex turned around to see those eyes staring at him in the gloom of his own bathroom.

"What, didn't I tell you, to..."

"Am I your slave Flex!"

His name sounded strange in her mouth - foreign, like he would have to earn it all over again or change it.

"I'm no slave," she continued, "my name's Hortence and I 'm no slave." Her eyes flashed again.

"All right," Flex said, "Hortence, chill, I accept you're no slave. You just scared the Jesus out of me! Let's come out of the bathroom okay?"

"Listen, that ain't goin' to do any good."

Flex looked down at his hands and he could still smell the
blood.

Hortence stepped right in front of him and took out her bottle,
splashing liquid on to his hands.

"All gone," she said, like a school matron.

Flex flicked the lights on, everything was a blur of white tiles
and designer mirrors. But the blood, the smell was gone.

And so was Hortence.

Flex switched the light off and stepped into the hallway, 'where
is she?' He thought, looking all around.

"Why I'm here," Hortence replied, standing in the same place
where Flex had left her and reading his mind. "I told you I
wouldn't move."

"You mean to say," Flex said, almost laughing, "that you didn't
follow me in there!"

"Why would I break my word Flex? Are you calling me a liar?"
And she stared at him with piercing eyes.

"Alright," Flex said, "as I told you I just need a haircut."

"You need much more than that, and it will cost you a thousand
pounds," Hortence replied and brushed the hair away from her
face. Her face had a rounded good-natured appeal, mixed with
a little of what looked like youthful exuberance. It was not the
kind of face Flex expected to find. But there was something
about the mouth, small, powerful, feminine and bold. The lips
full and the teeth all even and set back in her jaw. There was
something striking in the forehead brown and broad and of

course those eyes, little pools of black.

"No," Hortenece said, "You need a spiritual washout."

"Cha man, I've had enough of this!"

"What, do you want me to leave? Leave you in the state you're in. What with Colin's blood all over the place. And your spirit in tatters."

Flex sat down on his plush leather seats. He rubbed his forehead like an old man. "Alright, I need help," he said, "but just tell me, how do you know so much? Don't give me that spiritual insight business. I don't buy it. You know too much!"

"Okay Flex... I know Colin. I don't know him well. But I know him. He took a cab from the place that I work at in the evenings. I knew he was up to no good. And I know he's in hospital and you put him there, everybody knows, because you've got a big mouth. But do I have the gift? Yes! Are you sick? Yes! Can I help you? Yes!"

"Then do something then. My head is all busted up like a smashed melon. I'm pissed. I'm vexed and it ain't getting any better!"

"Alright chill! First stop smoking weed like a fool, it ain't going to relieve the pain!"

"I need something now," Flex said, looking around.

"You have a lot of gifts, but you've thrown them away."

"What do you mean?"

"I mean when this is done, there's a friend of yours that needs you. He needs your help."

"A friend? I don't have any friends?"

"Yes you do! Tayo!"

"What Righteous? How do you know him? That's one of your tricks in it? You know him right?"

"No," she replied sternly, "I saw his name."

"I knew it! Where on the table? You know I'm always leaving stuff about. Was it some old student union papers?"

"No I saw the name written in your heart."

 "Oh come on. I thought you were done pulling my leg!"

"I am. I saw it in your heart," she said and stared straight at him. Her eyes flashed red, black and just in the iris a little hint of green. The liquid blackness mixed with the power of deep melancholy power, sent a shudder of pure undiluted fear down Flex's spine and woke every part of his spiritual being, even the parts that he didn't know existed.

The longest day

Today is the longest day of the year. But the sun couldn't even penetrate the grey faded windows of the office. Grey and stale, the air was lifeless, even the plants were dying one by one and the people.

The phone rang incessantly and the email flicked continuously, 'you have new mail.' Tayo smiled when he thought of his new bulging bank account and frowned when he remembered that it was still only 11am.

'At least,' he smiled to himself, 'I'm going to see that new house. It's a snap at £250,000.' He had seven already and was after his eighth. He was earning £3,000 a week in rents alone from his tenants. 'Soon I'm going to have enough to retire. Retire at thirty- six. Now that would be great. Haven't I earned it?'

'I remember the last holiday I took, state of the art, the best apartment looking out at the beach of Negril. I remember partying so extravagantly that they thought I was a football star. But then any black with money must be a sportsman. I tried to explain that I dealt in commodities, finance and executive sales. But somehow it just didn't sink in. What do you mean? You do this after your training? I mean you're so big. Look at your muscles. 'It's strange,' Tayo thought. Then he remembered today was the day of his annual review. How had he allowed his mind to become distracted? He stood up and climbed the stairs, over four flights and then paced nervously outside. He was just in time.

Shortest hour...

Tayo stood waiting outside Simon's office. It was rare that
Simon actually did annual reviews himself. Tayo smiled to
himself. 'I expect the worse,' he thought, 'but what's he going to
do? I earned more money for him this month than anyone in
the entire company. What's he going to do?' Tayo paced up and
down the corridor. His shiny shoes making irregular sounds on
the very expensive mirrored floors. He sat down.

Tayo reflected on working for one of the most prestigious
companies in the entire Aldgate area. They made a weekly
turnover of 2 to 3 million and they prided themselves on their
profit, with a staff turnover to match.

'But when I left University,' Tayo thought with agitation, 'with
degrees in law and history, I had a mountain of righteous
indignation on my shoulders. At first I visited every black
organisation. I would sit there thinking, too much talk! Black
this, black that-conscious-nubian-righteous-kemetian-spiritual
words. But where is the action, these groups always say the
same thing, my sister, my brother, you've got to understand it
takes time to make change.' But Tayo thought, 'I don't want
anything big, just tangible. I went everywhere from church to
mosque, West Indian meeting hall, to African centred shrine.'

So Tayo had toyed with the idea of another country. And finally
he took the plunge, jumped in headfirst. For three years he
lived in Tanzania, reconnected the spiritual circle of his life, a
village outside Dar es Salaam, digging wells. He broke his back
in the sun, day in and day out, lost five stone and learnt
Swahili. Tayo would watch the sun dying on a full African
horizon. And then go to the local bar and order orange juice
and sit until the small morning, practising Swahili with the
local farmers.

Tayo fell in love with the land and learnt what it was like to irrigate a field and watch crops grow. 'Crop rotation keeps the land breathing!' He would smile every day as the sun spread across the horizon. A red sun on a green land with black thoughts.

At first he had been that big dumb foreigner, there were stares and sniggers. Somehow he seemed out of place. Perhaps it was his smell or the look, or the rhythm of his walk. He cut his hair, shaved his head and buried it under the largest and blackest tree he could find. He stopped shouting and started thinking, stopped thinking and started being. Then, eventually, the looks subsided; people would come up to him and start talking Swahili. From working with the earth he had become one with it - acculturalised.

But when Tayo talked Swahili the accent let him down. "You're not from here," they would say and shake their heads, "but good try," and they would sell to him at twice the price. But he got smart and with real economic savvy, he started getting the better deals. The farmers' wells got dug quicker, there were improvements, an encircling wall and new fields cleared. New irrigation tunnels and trees planted. New homes built. Tayo learnt, modified and developed. He was in seventh heaven.

A mobile phone blurted out a silly but catchy tune.

Tayo woke from his meditations.

He realised he was outside Simon's office in London, England, not Tanzania! No sun drenched landscapes, or clear blue skies - just bland grey ceilings. Tayo looked up and it seemed to stretch up forever, 'I swear these offices get bigger and bigger, but the minds get smaller and smaller.'

Meanwhile..

Simon, Tayo's boss, sat on his chair, in his office, playing on his phone like a child, pretending to be busy and all the while adjusting his thoughts. He sat down and bolt up right, sitting and looking at the chair that Tayo would be sitting in. Simon stood up and paced the room. 'That won't do,' he thought and sighed. He walked towards the blind and adjusted them, so a small beam of light would go straight into Tayo's eyes. He smiled and sat back in his chair.

He opened the drawer and flicked through the pages of 48 Laws of Power. He read to himself, 'Power must be absolute or it isn't power at all,' Henry Ireton. "True," Simon said and stretched himself out like a fat cat, doing up the buttons on his shiny new £450 waistcoat. Looking around his office and admiring for a while the minimalist art-deco furniture.

He used Feng Shui and Celtic runes to align every chair and book. He got rid of his ornate Chinese collision balls, (too much conflict) and the brass antique hourglass owned by Samuel Pepys now lay carefully wrapped and concealed in his drawer. (Time is too organic to be pressured into one minute of sand). He pulled up his Gucci socks and folded and unfolded his feet, checked the clock on his computer and then turned his computer off.

The seconds ticked by. The minutes passed. Still Simon waited. Twenty minutes, thirty. He resorted to doing the crossword to ease the time. And Tayo waited too, a thin line of perspiration broke out on his forehead, half in annoyance and half in anticipation.

Simon smiled and waited some more. Tapping his crocodile shoes on his newly finished floors and looking at his manicured fingernails, the smell of Clive Christian aftershave wafted through the room, 'that's enough, that's enough,' he thought.

"Listen, Sharon can you show him in." Simon said, speaking into his intercom.

Sharon, short skirt and no smile, a reject from every stereotyped black office woman that there has ever been, chewed gum and frowned at Tayo like he was a little boy.

"Don't go to sleep here," Sharon said frowning, "he'll sell, I mean see you now."

Tayo stared up at her, frowning back and pursed his lips together. He stood and nodded and sort of scowled, walked towards the door and opened it.

Simon stood and extended his hand, "Tayo, do come in," he said, "sorry to keep you waiting, I had a lot to do, come in take a seat."

Tayo stepped in and looked around, smelling the intimidation, it was rising high off the walls and sinking deep into the floors. The air was heavy with power, masculine white, sophisticated and cruel.

Tayo sat and felt the air strangling the oxygen from his lungs, the intense swirling of the fan methodically spinning and the sickly stench of some foul aftershave.

"I understand you're not happy," Simon said sitting and smiling at Tayo.

"I wouldn't say that." Tayo said trying to clear his throat and staring at Simon.

"Well there seems to be a lot of problems?"

"You mean with my report?"

"Well frankly yes."

"I just refused to sign it. I've been here some time you know and I think I've contributed quite a lot. I don't think that report reflects it."

"Well Tayo, you know I don't usually get involved in these matters, but to be honest I have been rather concerned by some things."

"What?" Tayo said, finally breathing and pushing the negative energy out of his lungs.

"Well you're not getting on are you," Simon said, slapping Tayo in the face with the brunt power of his spiritual strength and trying to drag his face in the dirt. The stench and the filth were overpowering. Battered and spiritually abused, Tayo reeled with pain and anguish. Simon slithered down Tayo's throat and tried to find the inner aspect of Tayo's core, nub, centre: the meridian of his absolute self, so that he could utterly destroy it.

"Listen Tayo, you've got to get on," Simon said, "it doesn't have to be like this. Listen, the issues you've got with your report and the appraisal **are real**. I know that you've done great work here. But nobody is going to give you credit, until they feel comfortable with you. You've got to! I don't care how you do it! You've got to make Mary feel comfortable with you! I don't care what you do."

Tayo wobbled only for a second. But his higher self drew light from the centre of the earth and mixed it with waters from the heavens. They all combined in his DNA. This was his rite of passage, his test.

"No," Tayo said. And his 'no' split the atoms within the DNA of his subconscious mind. His conscious, subconscious and unconscious became one. His hand and feet were filled with the power of love and he remembered, yes he remembered what he was.

"No," he said and his 'no' rumbled through the room like a mini earthquake.

"What do you mean? No!" Simon said, quivering a little and dropping all his little magic tricks in sheer fear.

"No." Tayo replied again and walked towards the blinds without asking, opening them. The light came in and filled the room with joy.

Simon winced and blinked, "What on earth are you doing?" He lost his temper and his anger replaced his reason. At the same time all his power dripped from his fingertips.

Tayo stared and watched Simon's power wane. He now looked so small, insignificant and irrelevant, like a very, very small boy.

Tayo smiled.

Simon had just enough energy to shakily mumble, "I'll expect your resignation, on my desk by tomorrow."

"Yes," Tayo said laughing and his laughter split the core of Simon's being and left a dishevelled mess.

Tayo stood up and bounced, yes bounced, like he used to bounce and his bounce, bounced him clear out of the room, clear out of the office and clear out of that World forever! He realised that Gunnislake was a rites of passage for the body.

That all the student politics had been a rites of passage for the mind. But now, only now, did he have a rites of passage for the spirit.

Now he was a man. And he smiled.

Eurocentric teaching

"So," Michael said, sitting and looking at Malika, "how can I help you?"

"I've put a complaint in against you," she replied, fidgeting with her hair.

Michael didn't look surprised, "yes and what for?"

"Your teaching method and style, I don't like it. I think you discriminate against the black students!"

"Why do you think I do that?" Michael replied, laughing and almost falling off his chair.

"Are you laughing at me?"

Michael looked at Malika's badly twisted locks and the poorly wrapped Kente cloth on her head. The fake foundation make up and the body shop lipstick, the childish and demure face, rounded naïve, yet pedantic and silly as well. The wide-eyed curiosity, mixed with immaturity, ambivalence and yes a slight trace of petulance.

'She's a fake,' he thought, 'with her fake head wrap and her fake Queen of Africa T shirt from Marks and Spencers. Her consciousness is a fashion accessory. It's November,' Michael thought, 'sandals, why the hell are you wearing sandals? You're a designer revolutionary for sure.' He wanted to laugh again and stopped himself, 'she looks like she's ten, when she's actually twenty-five! She behaves like she's five years old - but wants to be treated like she's sixty five!' This time he did laugh and he fell off his chair.

Malika stared at him in shock.

Michael regained his composure, "sorry about that, it's been a long day."

"I think your behaviour is really childish," Malika said and Michael wanted to laugh again but restrained himself.

"Listen I'm a big woman. I've been around a long time!"

"Really?" Michael said, not really intrigued but curious at least.

"I've been conscious for almost a year."

"Conscious, really for so long. But Miss Smith, it is Smith isn't it?"

"Yes Malika Smith."

"And how do you mean conscious, in what way conscious?"

"I haven't come here to discuss my development. I don't think you're any one to be discussing my development with."

"Really, why is that?"

"You're so white, Eurocentric, that's your problem!"

"Really," Michael said, "am I. What makes you say that?"

"First of all as I said, you're harder on the black students than you are on the white ones and the way that you teach the class. You're so smug. You sit their smiling and asking all these questions. If you know the answers, why don't you give them!?"

"You mean you don't know?"

"I mean you must think you're white. You stand up there so smug, smug, smug!! Why don't you just teach us? I paid my money for this course. I want my money's worth!"

"I think your really mixing three different things together," Michael replied coolly, "the first is regarding the curriculum, the second is regarding teaching style. The latter and the more serious accusation is regarding differential treatment. With the first matter, I would take that up with Director of Studies. I think you'll find that I stick quite closely to the curriculum as stated in the Prospectus. But you are welcome to contact him. I'll give you his number. As for the second matter: the style of my teaching. Not every student is going to like everybody's teaching style. You don't have to like me, because I don't have to like you. But we are both here to do a job. As regards the third matter, there is no differential treatment and certainly you are not treated harsher because of the colour of your skin. That's not how I work. But if you want to discuss this matter further, I would suggest you take it up with the highest authority, the head of this institution."

"If there is nothing else, can I ask you please to leave my office."

"What! Who do you think you are?" Malika said, almost spluttering, "I just wanted to talk to you, I don't like the way you teach!"

"No Malika, you don't like the truth that I teach. It awakens your own truth and it makes you feel insecure about the World. Now, if you had come in here for true help. I would have given it to you. You know some coping mechanisms. I would and can still help."

"I don't need your help. You're just like all the rest!" And with that she stood up and walked out, slamming his office door. "That's one's messed up girl," Michael said under his breath. "One messed up girl."

Affirmations

Tayo was reading and thinking.

'For a long time,' Tayo thought, 'I've allowed myself to drift so far from who I am? Or what I yet may be. Like a river diverted from the great sea, the sea and hope of its immortal self. To live forever in the divine fulfilment of one's true destiny, that's the purpose of I, the ego, the sum being of one's internal path. But like a warrior with amnesia, I've slipped from my destiny and lost myself in the convenience of the now! I forgot who I was. How could I allow ordinariness to cheat me of my reincarnated birthright! No more! I will be that which I am. I will be more than mere man! Nothing can stop the unstoppable truth of one's own heart. Feel the rhythm of my heart and the beat of my soul, as it screams and yells to be heard amongst all the mediocrity of modern civil-lie-sation.'

'I cannot stop the wheel now it turns. I cannot go back to the middle aged spread of 2.4 and white picket fences. I cannot allow apathy and indifference to destroy my own African nature, the spirit of me and I and you. I would rather be buried alive than not live like a man. Watch and behold the recombination of Tayo Akinjo. I have died and been reborn and my rebirth will be so bright that the sun will fade under my light. I swear undiluted and complete love, to restore the axis of the world back in place. Watch and learn how a child becomes a man.'

Tayo went back to his reading and thought, 'black extremism is fake, like the word black revolutionary. All black people have ever wanted is human rights. There are no extremists on the black side. Humanism has always been the order of the day, even for the most so-called radicals. Show me a black nationalist and I'll show you an ordinary human being. But show me a white nationalist and I'll show you genocide!

Because prejudice plus **power** equals genocide. Tayo stood on his legs like a restless lion about to become a dragon and he surveyed his books.

Tayo dived into the centre of the World. He was knee deep in books, words, words and words. Lies, lies and here and there the truth mixed with lies and still he kept reading. Page after page, pouring through the obscure and the mundane, the common place and the ordinary. Until at last, he read, "Before you speak, ask yourself, is it kind, is it necessary, is it true, does it improve on the silence." He flicked through another book, "the body is false, and so are its fears, Heaven and hell, freedom and bondage. It is all invention. What can they matter to us? We are awareness itself" and he examined the cover, "interesting," he read on, "it is but few who hear about the Self, fewer still dedicate their lives to its Realization. Wonderful is the one who speaks about the Self; rare are they who make it the supreme goal of their lives." He thought, 'I'll absorb the memory of this reality, what I have read here and I'll mix it with the inner contemplation of my mind, unmixed. I'll fix it to the sticking part of my soul. I won't intellectualise it, I'll use it to feed my soul,' and he smiled, not smugly, but knowingly.

Mirrors

Dionne Douglass had been staring into mirrors for months, slowly picking herself apart. The physical wounds healed. Even the perforation of her womb through the miscarriage and the fact that she could never have children - all healed. The pain of the ruptured spleen - healed. Her bones had been reset and the skin was sewn together. But the mental and spiritual scars went deeper - they wouldn't heal.

She rubbed aloe vera into her body. And examined her complexion. 'I'm just a little lighter than my mother,' she thought, 'my complexion seemed so perfect before, but now I want to be darker, a lot darker.' She lit her candles. She sat for a moment, taking out her coloured contact lenses and staring at her own eyes. She looked ten years older. She wanted to cry, but the tear ducts had worked too hard. There were no tears left.

She stared at her artificial eyebrows drawn in lines above her eyes and she wiped them off with a tissue. She looked at her funky brownish red lipstick and felt disgusted.

She looked at the rouge on her cheeks and pulled off her fake eyelashes, throwing them on the floor.

She wiped it all off....

Dionne was looking for the real her, underneath the she that she had fashioned for herself.

She looked at her hair, months of neglect and her real hair was growing in tufts. Her scalp was itchy and she picked up the scissors and started to cut. At first tentatively and then voraciously. Lumps and piles of the fake stuff fell in heaps around her.

At last her natural hair stood out. She stared in the mirror.

"That's better," she said, "but it's still not enough."

She reached inside her drawer and pulled out an electric shaver. And she started to shave. The hair came away easily and she felt the smoothness of her scalp. "I've never ever seen my own head before!" she said, rubbing it.

She kept on shaving until her scalp was gleaming and finally she looked in the mirror, and she smiled. "Now truly," she said to herself, disrobing and walking over to the shower and turning on the water, "truly," as the water touched her skin, "I have been born again."

The water soaked her skin and entered every pore: guilt, ignorance and anger ran down the plughole with the dirty water, gurgling and frothing.

She wiped the perspiration off the mirror and stared at herself, scars and all. She looked at the contours, colours and shades of her skin from blue black, to brownish red. She looked at her two-tone lips, the top lip dark and the bottom one almost red. She looked at the almost conical shape of her head pointing to heaven. She looked at the Africaness of her soul and for the first time ever she fell in love with herself.

Love, Love, Love II

Tyronne Thomas was sitting with his thighs far apart, so his ass would fill up the seat and it did. He smiled like a stupid fat cat who had just got his cream. His teeth were perfect white and his nails perfect manicures. He played with the lead of his phone. "I'm a black man init, every Blackman knows how to play football init," he said. "If you don't know how to play then you ain't really black," he was speaking loudly into his phone, it was hands free. He pushed the gear stick into fourth and put his foot down on the accelerator.

"Yeah I've got real style," he boasted, looking at himself in the mirror. "I took it past three players and I didn't even break into sweat. That nigga (in a village just outside Zaire, an old African man who had been teaching his people for a hundred years died when he heard that N word and his ancient knowledge died with him) didn't know what to do. I start trials today you know, yeah with the seniors. It's my first day. Yeah I'll be rolling in pure bills. I'm off there now and I'm bare early. I hate getting there early. I want to make my entrance init. I'll **show** them who the star is init. I'll be getting pure bills you know! I've got pure skills. I'm going college init. I'm going college too init. Yeah yeah, yeah! I'll be getting pure bills. You know I've got my flat and everythin', I brought my new car init. It's a BMW 5 series. I'm driving it now. Yeah, yeah.." His taut   muscular thighs tightened and untightened as he maneuvered down the motorway.

He cruised down the A 406 at a hundred miles an hour. And then.

Suzie wobbled!

Tyronne almost lost control of his car.

She was a full fifty metres away, on the pavement. But she wobbled. He felt the vibrations down his spine.

"What was that?" Tyronne said.

He stopped the car abruptly in the middle of the motorway.

The car behind swerved to miss him, and the one behind that came to an abrupt stop.

"I'll talk to you later," Tyronne mumbled, ignoring the honking of horns, abuse and confusion behind him. He gave a toothy grin as he caught sight of the object of his affection. He slipped the car into first and then second, did a three point turn at full speed. He slipped off the motorway - even as the drivers in the cars behind swore and yelled at him. Tyronne was so ecstatic he almost drove onto the pavement. He opened the car door and stared at a wide-eyed Suzie adjusting her flimsy blouse.

"Get in," Tyronne said.

She smiled and looked up and down the street.

"My, so forceful," she said, stepping closer and looking at his cock.

He opened his thighs even more, (if that's possible). She wobbled over to the passenger door. "This looks brand new," she said, "you must be rolling in it!"

"I'm a footballer init," Tyronne said.

"Really," Suzie said, almost wetting herself with excitement and forgetting all about her terrible rejection in the bank seven months ago, (she was still in therapy: pub crawls and male strippers). 'Here is a real black man,' she thought.

Three hours later...

Suzie smoked a cigarette, and looked at Tyronne's **taught** buttocks.

"Yeah," he mumbled.

"You want something stronger?"

"Yeah why not," Tyronne mumbled again, looking at her blue eyes and drowning in those aqua pools of cyanide.

"That's a good boy," Suzie said slapping his ass. He giggled like a seven year old with his mother.

He took the spliff from her hand and inhaled long drags and there, in the midst of the haze, he remembered, 'I've got my senior trials today.'

"Chill," Suzie said, watching him, as he tried desperately to get dressed, "they know who the star is."

"Yeah, yeah, but I'm two hours late!" He said looking at his watch, "besides what's your name. I don't even know what your name is?"

"My name's Suzie," she said, "listen you know where I live, any time you want to come and I do mean come, give me a call and let me know. But call me first. You know I've got a boyfriend. He can be a real pig."

"Yeah I can handle him," Tyronne said flexing his biceps.

"No," Suzie said, suddenly seriously, "he can be a bastard, but he's a **real man**! I mean you're sweet and all - I mean cute (seeing the confusion on his face.) Anyway, let's meet soon.

Here's my number." (She wrote it on a piece of paper and stuffed it in his pocket, accidentally feeling him up as she did it.)

Tyronne smiled, comforted and pulled on the rest of his clothes, bouncing towards his car.

He was now three hours late.

Later that day....

"Yeah Tyronne, Tyronne Thomas isn't it? You did okay in the trials, even though you were late. Your agent said your mother had to go to hospital. Is she okay?" the coach said, staring at Tyronne's blood shot eyes.

"Yeah, yeah," Tyronne said, looking at his agent, an inquisitively sharp and sophisticated looking man, with a vindictive streak running all the way down his back.

"But you know," the coach said, "we have random drug testing now. It is a requirement of selection. Your agent said you're a clean living guy, so it shouldn't be a problem. We're going to need some of your blood and urine right away. Okay?!"

Tyronne looked at the floor and then sheepishly at his agent, as his whole fake world of fast cars and loose women, champagne and designer suits fell to pieces around him. No more rolling in women with their own condominiums, no more being better than the average black. No more boasting and bragging. No more escapes down the false gaslight of an artificially constructed bright light. His whole World was at an end. And he didn't know any other world to hide in.

Tramp

She stood there covered in urine. Her pants sticking to her thighs and they stank and she stank. Her teeth were yellow and she muttered and screamed occasionally to herself and at the passing cars that raced towards her.

"Bloody blacks, black men, bloody black bastards!"

Michael was early this morning for work. He was bouncing along until he saw her. He stared. There was something about the shape of the face and the eyes - yes the eyes seemed all too familiar. Then there was the Kente cloth wrap.

"My God," Michael said under his breath, "that's Malika! What are you doing?"

She looked up at him, mad.

"What. Get away from me you black bastard!"

Michael stepped closer, "What happened, why haven't you been to class. What happened?"

She looked at him and stumbled back.

"Piss off," she said, spitting at him.

Michael wiped the spit off his face unperturbed, "come with me, come on."

She stared at him wildly, "Paedophile, you're a paedophile, all black men are paedophiles, look at him!" she was gesturing to a man on the street who was going into a newsagents. "He's a paedophile!" she screamed, pointing at Michael.

"What," the man said, rubbing the redness out of his eyes.

"He's a filthy nonce, a child molester," she yelled.

The man took a step forward and was joined by a younger abler associate, Mark Braithwaite. He'd been stacking fruit on his stall just adjacent to the street. A local gossip called Marjorie Smithe joined in.

"There's all sorts coming in the country now, since they relaxed the immigration laws. I blame the government," Marjorie muttered, "most of them have got Aids too!!"

Mark Braithwaite rolled up his sleeves.

Michael surveyed the scene. A small crowd was now staring at him. Malika was shrieking like a Banshee, "Paedophile, paedophile!!!!!!"

He stepped back and turned down a nearby street, stepping into a slight trot. Before stopping. He sighed, "try to do some good and end up a victim. Not this time. Not this time around. We don't need any more victims."

Michael felt a tap on his shoulder.

He turned and turned again, as a white gnarled fist came flying towards his head and narrowly grazed his forehead.

It was Mark Braithwaite.

The Full splits

That morning and every morning for ten years

Since Michael had given up weed, he was born again. Not in church or the mosque, but yes, like Lazarus he had risen from the dead.

He could do the full splits now and felt the blood in his toes in the mornings. There was no more grogginess or sleepy mornings. Every day he was up at the crack of dawn, three mile run and exercise, he used to laugh at Tayo, but now he cultivated his health as a divine aspect of his own being. He had had, a male epiphany. But there was no road to Damascus, for his divine rebirth, only the concrete tenements of South London.

He could touch his toes without coughing and clear a flight of steps without breaking into a sweat. He was back on the pads in his basement and shadowboxing every morning before University. But he yearned to practice on a live body, to test his divinity in the fires of conflict.

Dancing on the street

"What?" Michael scowled, dancing around like a much younger man, adjusting his glasses and tie like a black secret agent.

Mark Braithwaite spat, "you filthy bastard, you lot should have your balls cut off!"

Michael smiled, and looked around for the rest of the crowd, calmly kicking Mark in his chest.

Mark stumbled and fell, one hand on the ground and another on his chest. "I'll get you back for that, you nonce!"

"Where's the rest of your friends?" Michael muttered, bouncing up to him.

"I don't need anyone to teach filth like you a lesson!!"

"Oh, that's music to my ears," Michael replied, kneeing him in his chest, and stepping back to look at his handy work. "You know," Michael continued, dancing around him, like a ballerina and a prize-fighter all rolled into one, "working out on the bag, it's just not the same, sometimes you need a live dummy. You know you would look much better with my fist in your face!"

"What you talking about?"

"I said," Michael replied, avoiding a punch and elbowing him in his head, "that I am really going to enjoy hurting you."

But Mark wasn't listening, there was blood coming from his nose and he was out cold, (no more dancing for him tonight.)

Michael felt Mark's pulse, "I'd better make sure." He sighed, "good," and looked around, "nobody around either and no camera. Today is a good day."

Michael did up his tie again, straightened his glasses and walked calmly away. He hadn't even broken into a sweat.

Mark Braithwaite's eyes flickered, as he regained a little consciousness.

"Next time," Mark mumbled, splitting blood, "next time, I'm going to shoot you and then cut off your balls."

But Michael's balls were comfortably in his pants, in his trousers and firmly attached to his person *(long may they remain so)*, as he walked towards Borough station.

But then Michael remembered Malika and a sadness came over him. He wept, 'just two weeks, is that all it takes? I'll never laugh at anyone in distress again. And some how I'm going to help her!'

The House of Fun

Kwame Aja's fall had been as ignominious as his rise.

"This is a real house of fun, nothing but fun everywhere," Kwame mumbled. He stank. And his piss coated the sheets and the floor of the observation room where he slept.

They got so tired of his urinating, that they only cleaned him up twice a week.

In the mornings he would walk out of his room stark naked, wash, brush his teeth and then stand in the corridor displaying his body for all the nurses and patients. He saw it as his one method of defiance.

The staff pretended not to notice. But somehow at 9am there were always more female staff on the ward than usual.

Expectant!

Waiting!

Then he stepped out.

As God made him, but not as God intended!

Naked! Cock swinging, balls dangling. They all stared at his genitals through the comfort of the glass windows. Miss Smith the supervisor even adjusted her glasses. It was better than reality TV!

Kwame stood there hands on hips. Then he bounced into the bathroom, wiggling his buttocks like a showgirl stripper on a stage. The only difference was he wasn't getting paid. No, his performance was for free, every morning, of every day. The only cost was his immortal soul.

And just like every day and every morning when he had
finished his absolutions, he stepped inside his room and pissed
all over his bed and sat in it. The stench wafted all the way
down the corridor. It was as regular as the sun rising.

This day however was different. Rumours had circulated about
Kwame's predicament and now Tayo pulled up at the hospital.
He put the gear of his car into neutral. He stepped out onto the
street, centrally locking it. He bounced towards the hospital and
stood at the front desk.

"I'm looking for the Canaan Ward." Tayo said forcefully, staring at a nurse who was half asleep.

"What?" she replied in a Polish accent and almost turned to
leave.

"I'm looking for the ward known as Canaan, it's a mental health
ward and I know it's part of this hospital and unless you start
co-operating, we'll both end up there!"

She stared at him and made some gesture down the corridor.
Tayo stared, frowned and walked. The antiseptic stench was
overpowering and yet strangely hypnotic, like the songs of
mermaids to sailors, as they crashed their ships against rocks to
pursue them.

Tayo found every step getting heavier. He sighed, "At last."
The Canaan Ward sign loomed up.

He stepped and walked down a corridor, which seemed to go
on forever. Forever nowhere. But nowhere came to an end at
last.

The smell changed, not to Dettol but urine. Piss. The kind that had fermented and turned into something else fouler and more poisonous: Despair. "What a smell," Tayo said, "it smells like someone has died."

He looked at the sign. It contained a roster with all the names and all the rooms. But the stench almost blinded his vision.

Tayo looked down the list. At last he saw the name. "Kwame Aja," he read it out loud, "Observation room."

Tayo bounced down the corridor, though the smell was dripping from the walls in puddles of melancholy.

Tayo stood outside the door. He knocked. No answer and he turned the latch. The smell was so strong that he almost fell over.

Kwame Aja lay on the floor naked in a pool of his own urine, with a soaking wet sheet around his legs.

Tayo shook his head, "Kwame is that you.... are you okay?"

Kwame half lifted his head and nodded.

"Cover yourself up man," Tayo said.

Kwame just stared at him.

"Someone should clean this up," Tayo said looking around, "this is wrong!"

Tayo stood and shouted outside the door, "hey I think this patient needs help?"

"There's no point," Kwame said, "they clocked you, they won't come 'till tomorrow."

"So you can talk!" Tayo said, "have you no respect!" and he
pulled out a blanket from the side of the room and threw it over
his naked body.

Kwame looked at Tayo and the glaze disappeared from his
eyes. "I'm not a man, I can't feel God in me any more," he
mumbled and wept.

"What do you mean," Tayo replied?

"They've stripped me of my myself."

"No only you can do that," Tayo replied.

"I've got no will left. I can't feel light in my hands anymore!"

Tayo looked at him, "the Creator is in honour, respect and
courage, these are the noble parts of our will. But the Creator is
also in the simple things, breath and thought. So long as you
have thought you can make the World. Remember the World
was made with word, and the word is a living, breathing thing.
So long as you can have a thought you are divine."

Kwame turned his head for a while, like he was listening to a
far off song - but had forgotten the tune, "yes," he said, "so
long as I can think, I am." And he wept.

The tears welled up in Tayo's eyes and they both cried like
brothers.

At last the bell sounded and the waiting time came to an end.

They came. They shut the doors. They locked him up.

Kwame stood at his window staring behind the lines in the glass, like the bars of a cell.

"England has eaten me. There's nothing left but bits! But they want you, you know, and they're coming to you through us. But don't let them win," Kwame mouthed through the glass.

Tayo turned and stepped away, wiping the tears from his face. "How many more, how many more. Hell, hell, hell, hell, hell, hell, hell!!!!!!!"

He turned a corner and walked up to the front desk, the same nurse was there. She stared at him like a wounded animal.

"Listen can you show me who's in charge? I want to make a complaint! **Who the hell is in charge here!!!**" Tayo shouted.

Physical Jerk

A week later...

Tayo was doing his learning by numbers, he undid the lace of his trainers and pulled them on, but the inlets were filthy. The sky was as red as blood. He pulled his black socks up and standing, skipped over the rickety fence, bleached from the sun of a temporary momentary summer, which waxed and waned too soon. Lifting his heels he almost flew, he yawned and the brown grass turned green. He stretched, reaching for the blue sky, but he couldn't reach the Sun yet. He looked at the street sign held on by its rivets. A bird had crapped on it and left a stain. "Empire Road," Tayo read scowling, as the white crap dripped off it, "Empire Road indeed!"

And he ran down streets, and was jostled by Polish and Russian workers fighting to turn English. He ran down backyards, through parks and onto hills. He went down familiar and unfamiliar paths, until at last he stood on an outcrop of hill and stared.

'This is something new?' he thought still staring. There in the bushes, a series of broken rocks and here and there, part of a wall and roof. 'Where's this place? It's still Southwark' and he checked the postcode on a nearby street.

He smiled.

He stepped closer, standing in the ruins. He was glistening with sweat and surveyed the scene.

He fell in love and closed his eyes so that the love could spread. There amongst the red brick ruins he could see the future. 'Over there would be the Saturday school. Over here the study classes, there the business classes, a greenhouse over here and we'd grow some vegetables there. And over here and there.'

'Karibu Nyumba,' Tayo thought instinctively and checked his watch, 'for years now, I'm been drifting with the tide. Now it's time to begin to turn it.'

He looked at his watch and made a mental note to check for this location on the World Wide Web.

'But for now goodbye,' Tayo thought.

Tayo ran eight more miles, sweated, spat, groaned, washed and brushed his teeth. It wasn't even six am.

Meanwhile in a 'high class' part of London.

"Tayo, who does he think he is?" Clinton mumbled, as he rolled over. "Who the hell does he think he is?" He kicked his stained bed sheets and rolled over. His toenails were black with grime, the funk of not washing for two weeks. His hair was an unkempt Afro with bits of bedding in it. Clinton rolled over and rolled out a spliff. "I need something to wake me up, life's getting harder, harder by the second." He opened the draw and looked at his police badge, (was it real, was it really his!). He kissed his yellow teeth like he was waiting for an encore.

Rubbing his groin and pulling his pants over his arse, Clinton stood and gawped at the mirror. "Getting old," he said. He examined the scar on his forehead, "memories, everybody needs memories, Gunnislake that's the place. How could I forget?"

Clinton stood at the sideboard and inspected a hanging Guyanese flag, "beautiful," he said, "all those beautiful colours." He broke wind, rubbed his groin again. He had acquired three sexually transmitted diseases last year alone,

from twenty different women and then promptly spread it to
about twenty more.

The bathroom window grimy with steam and dirt masked his
entrance, even when he dribbled his way in, finished his daily
duties and swallowed a mouth full of blue rinse mouthwash. He
spat it out, mostly on himself and ambled his way back into the
front room. He opened, 'Thus Spoke Zarathustra,' at page 28.
"Interesting," Clinton said farting again, "very interesting."
And he picked up his phone and dialled the familiar digits.

Meanwhile...

Tayo clenched his knuckles in the oblivion of the dusk as it
turned into morning and he sighed. He felt his phone vibrating.

He released his hands and turned it on.

"Yep, who is it?"

"An old friend?"

"Re...ally, who?"

Pause.

"It's Flex."

"Flex how you doing? How did you get my number?"

"There's always a way?"

Tayo paused, "so what have you been doing? **Who are you**
these days?"

"Well,....." Flex said.

"No don't tell me who you are. What you are speaks so loudly that I can't hear you," Tayo replied.

Flex paused again, not knowing what to say.

"It's all right," Tayo continued, "you know I spoke to Michael recently, it must be for a reason. We three can do some good. You're looking for a hopeless cause to find absolution, yeah, well. I think I just found one. Meet me...But tell me something Flex, do you think God's still keeping score, anymore?"

Flex hesitated, "No, I think She lost count, long, long ago."

Breaking waters

"You were all born originals, don't turn yourself into a copy,"
Tayo said, rubbing his baldhead and parking the car. "However
we got here, whatever twist and turn, it is not by chance. It is
not anymore the youthful exuberance of disaffected youth. We
are men now. We'd better have some substance to support us, or
the next generation of youth will reject us, as we rejected those
who went before. Anything to say?"

"Nah," Flex said, opening the car door.

"Nothing, so long as we don't have to make speeches. I'm tired
of speeches," Michael added, rubbing his baldhead and undoing
his safety belt.

"Follow me. Come with me," Tayo said, shutting the door of
his car, looking around and leading them through a series of
bushes and up a hill.

"There is a place. It's high and looks down on most of South
London and it is surrounded by green. When the Sun sets it
seems to fill up the sky. Look, see for yourself," he added.

They stood on an outcrop of hill and the Sun rose, filling the
World with light, as if it was the very first day.

"I don't know who owns this place." Tayo said, "Or how we
can get it. But I'm sure we could find out. This could be our
start, something tangible. And we could run stuff from here.
But this time it will be our place. No student rules, or fears of
this and that. It will be our place," and he leant on a nearby
fence and smiled like a cat.

Flex rubbed his newly shaved head and half smiled, "So what's
the catch? Do we just need money?"

"Yeah," Michael added, laconically, "there has to be a catch."

"There is," Tayo replied, "I did some research and this land is up for redevelopment. They're going to build expensive condominiums. It'll look like yuppie heaven. There won't be any green here either. Apparently it's one of the few places in South London that you will be able to see the Olympic village from. This is a prime site. If we can get it, it will be like opening up a window in the centre of the World and letting the light in."

"This is going to mean a lot of council meetings," Flex said.

"And money, even if we manage to get the nod and defeat all the housing developers, then we've still got to build. It's going to cost millions," Michael added, adjusting his button down shirt.

"I agree," Tayo said, "if it was easy, what would be the fun in that!"

Michael frowned.

Abdul Hasim

Abdul skipped down the stairs of his three-bedroom house and just missed the dog excrement, which had been chucked there the night before (he had enemies everywhere). It wasn't really his house but the council had given up trying to evict his family. It was probably because he was a rising star. Who would have thought that Abdul would be the Tower Hamlet's answer to Malcolm X and Martin Luther King all rolled into one.

Why Abdul was the smartest kid on the block! At age fourteen he had got the other kids in the neighbourhood to work for him, not selling drugs but raising money for a new mosque and community centre. It had taken them three years but they had done it. It was now the centre of the community. He was respected, liked and more than that, trusted. A year ago he had got all the local businesses to pull together and invest in the local school. Their investment had increased so much that they now almost owned the place. Lessons in Urdu and English, the history of Bangladesh and Pakistan, seats on the board of Governors, the school was 89% Asian and rising.

Abdul was lean, hungry, tired but fed up. He liked the reputation of the community leader but hankered after the street cred of a playboy. And a white playboy at that! He loved partying and women, any women, any women at all, so long as they were fit. But he hated himself for loving the smell of sex, more than he loved the smell of success.

He hated himself for partying all night and waking up with a different woman of a different colour, with different hair and a different face and in a different room. It was too much difference. Now all he wanted was someone who was the same, the same as him! He cursed his inadequacy and lack of cultural fibre, his weakness gnawed at him from the inside. He was getting sick. His asthma was getting worse like a disease.

Abdul's little sister grabbed his arm, and pulled him towards the open door.

"No more sweets Misbah," he said.

"Oh come on please, please!" She had a way of begging which sounded like an order.

"No, do you know what they put in sweets?"

"I don't care, I like 'em!"

"Like them or not, you ain't going to get 'em!"

"You'd better!"

"I'd better?!"

"Or I'm goin' to tell Mummy that I saw con...do..ms in your room!"

"What, who told you that word?" Abdul said.

"Yeah and I've got some here," she said reading, "Look, ribbed raspberry flavoured with extra lub...r..ic..ation!"

"Give that here," Abdul shouted snatching it, "now listen, you just behave!" He reached inside his pocket and pulled out three pounds.

"Look, go and get some chocolate, keep the change."

"Okay brother thank you," Misbah said, innocently.

Abdul sighed and rubbed his forehead.

Friends and enemies

Tayo skipped out of bed, "Just sixty press ups and sit ups, and a little stretching for today." He sweated and groaned but **didn't** look at himself in the mirror. Brushing his teeth and bathing, perhaps he was learning to live without vanity as his friend or · perhaps he was just busy, or both. He dressed, some ordinary brown slacks, a grey jumper and a black jacket, nothing outlandish, everything just practical, just like the frown on his forehead.

He skipped down the steps two at a time and the Sun was shining. The dogs had been out early and left the pathways fouled, but Tayo skipped past it, over the cracks in the pavement and a dead pigeon.

He jumped on a bus spurning his car and rode the 45 all the way down to Elephant and Castle. The bus was deathly quiet, except for a boy at the back with a head like a chessboard, trying and failing to put graffiti on the back window with a crayon.

Tayo pounced onto the street and across the alleyway into Tom's Internet café. Abdul was sitting there getting his head together.

"You're early," Tayo said.

"So are you." Abdul said looking at his watch, "at last I get to meet you. They always talk about you in hushed whispers. I think they're still scared of you."

"Me, that was over a decade ago,"Tayo said sitting.

"I'm telling you though, the stuff you did was an inspiration."

"It was nothing, really. I mean it was nothing. We should have been smarter."

"But I heard there were lots of you then. I mean a proper organisation."

"I wouldn't say that."

"Well. So how can I help you? I mean I can hardly believe it. I'm asking you, how I can help you."

"Well you read my email didn't you?"

"I didn't understand it though."

"What I said is that I would like us to work together. You know we're trying to buy a derelict building. It's on a hill where you can see all of South London. The place has massive potential. At first nobody was interested in it. But now everybody wants a piece of it, including the council."

"Typical, they're the same in Tower Hamlets."

"That's my point. I'm not talking about a grand alliance or anything, I mean all the people of colour unite thing died in the 1980's with the loony left councils. But we have got some common objectives."

"But I don't understand. I'm in Tower Hamlets and you're down in Brixton and Peckham."

"That's the point. We know you are the single most important figure amongst Asian youth in this country."

"Who's we?"

"I mean my friends and I."

"Your friends?"

"Yes that's right."

"What friends. You mean you've got a black organisation going. That's interesting, because to be honest you're not dealing from a position of strength."

"What do you mean?"

"Now I respect you. But most black people I wouldn't give them the time of day. Most of your men are just interested in getting white women and acting tough. They're not interested in anything constructive, they think they're gangsters. They'd sell themselves for money. As for your women, Asian women would never behave how yours do. Yesterday I heard one farting on the bus and then boasting about how many men she'd screwed. That's your community, it's in a mess! I mean black people are really in a state. Have you been on the bus recently, have you seen the state your people are in?"

Tayo didn't answer but knew in his heart there was some truth in it.

Abdul continued, "when my parent's came here, black people used to laugh at us. I mean at the way we used to speak our language. Some of them would say why don't you speak English? That's why the people here don't like you, cause you keep yourself to yourself with your own culture. And you keep your women and your children at home. Haven't you heard of equal rights? They said you need to integrate if you're going to get on. Black people used to laugh at us all the time and they reckoned we wouldn't survive. But now in 2006, twenty three years later, whose laughing?"

Tayo shrugged his shoulders.

"We're laughing. And we're laughing at you. Why shouldn't we, you laughed at us! I mean sometimes blacks used to join in with whites to attack Asians. That ain't going to happen now is it! Whatever you do with your building and your organisation, it's already too late. Your people are finished. I know about culture. I'm a Bengali Muslim from Brick Lane. How more cultured can you get?"

"I don't disagree with anything that you said," Tayo replied thinking, "except the finished bit. It ain't over until it's over. And it ain't over yet!"

Abdul smiled.

Tayo continued, "listen I'm not looking for a rainbow alliance. All I'm saying is check your contacts in South London. I heard you had connections in the council."

"Yes so?"

"So we're going to need your help."

"I don't know?"

"All I'm asking is think about it. Do what you can. Remember it's always good to have friends."

"I've already got more friends than I need. No this won't be for friendship," And he stood to leave, "no this will be charity."

"Whatever," Tayo said smiling, "but remember that nothing ever stays the same. The World turns to remind us that change is inevitable."

"Let's hope you can afford to wait." Abdul said, shaking hands with Tayo and skipping out onto the street, "take care."

"We ain't waiting for anything," Tayo muttered quietly under his breath, as he watched him go, "we're taking what we need now. With or without your help!" And he bit his lip and ordered an orange juice from an increasingly expectant waitress that had been eyeing him and listening (rather intently) to their conversation. She shuffled rather rapidly to his table, depositing a rather murky glass on it.

Tayo eyed the contents of his glass and decided against drinking. He looked out of the window and caught sight of his own people fronting and playing and thought, 'but he's right though, it really doesn't look good.'

Meetings and More meetings

Tayo and Michael surveyed the Council Chamber. "I thought you were going to get people," Tayo said to Michael.

"I tried," Michael replied, "people promised, whether they come or not is another matter," and he rubbed his bald head, "what about your lawyer friends?"

"Yeah he said he would be late."

"He? I thought we we're talking about we!"

"No. There is no we. That was fifteen years ago. Now it's just he!"

"Looks like it will be like old times then."

"Yeah," Tayo replied, "we're going to have to disrupt this meeting all by ourselves."

"Yeah, but it drives me out of my mind."

"Your mind! No, smell the air and your can smell your mind in the air. Look up beyond the roof of this stinking sanatorium of despotic misrule and see the Sun. See your mind in it. Look up and see the Moon rising to its ultimate zenith and see you're there, mixed in with the energies of female transformation and restoration. Look beyond the heavens and the clouds, to the ultimate pinpoint at the centre of the divine nub of the universe and see your mind is there. You are everywhere and everything is you. So long as you are in yourself, you can never be out of yourself."

"Have you finished?"

"Yeah."

"When I said what I said. I said it euphemistically. I don't mean I'm actually out of my mind. It's a figure of speech you know. Enough. So let's earn our names!" He stood and Tayo followed. They didn't even break into a sweat, as they clambered down the stairs and stood at the nape of the entrance that **wound** its way to the stage.

Michael frowned and Tayo smiled.

But Flex was there. They smelt him before they saw him.

"You took your time," Tayo said, "have you done it?"

"Better than that, I found a few friends of yours, they said they were lost."

Abdul skipped in behind him.

"I thought your weren't coming," Tayo said, smiling.

"A promise is a promise," Abdul replied.

"Have you got a plan? Because I'm all out! We were going to disrupt the meeting. They've been filibustering for the last three hours!"

Abdul smiled, "don't worry about it, sit down," he said. "Just remember that you'll owe me one."

"Yeah," Tayo replied a little confused, but sitting down nevertheless.

"I've brought my mum and my sister," motioning behind him for his mum to follow him.

"You're Mum!" Michael laughed, staring at him and remembering him from his class at University.

"Just sit!" Abdul said, "I didn't know my teacher would be here (looking at Michael) but now it's my time to teach."

Abdul's mother and sister promptly arrived with no pomp and little circumstance, quietly sitting in the front row and staring upwards at the stage where the council sat.

Tayo looked at Flex, "did you manage to get all the depositions."

"Yeah I've got them here with the signatures. I went to my friends on the streets and got them to sign, saying, you know there's no community centre in the area and all that, you know the stuff."

"Michael have you got the statistical returns?"

"Yeah I've got them, they're all here. Plus reports about crime in the area and the lack of after school projects and how these programmes can decrease truancy and criminal behaviour, mentoring and the need for positive role models etc. He brandished an attaché case which he had put by the back of the wall."

"You won't need any of that?" Abdul said eavesdropping, "watch!"

The Mayor sat in his regal robes. His name was Azam Khan and up to that point he had been less than interested in the proceedings. He had noticed the presence of three black men in the chamber. He knew why they were there. And he had no intention of discussing their matter today or any other day! There were very few things that he didn't know about in his

council. 'Community centre, community centre, what the area
doesn't need is another community centre! What we do need to
do is attract a different class of person, who can bring money
in,' he thought distracted and annoyed.

Azam Khan held his office by the smallest majority. Being
neither Labour nor Conservative, he walked the pathway
between right and left and always came up with a pragmatic
centre. 'After all South London isn't Tower Hamlets. No this
area is a melting pot, there's no community here. I come from a
community and there's none here!' He thought adjusting his
robes of office, 'we've done enough black things this year,
Multicultural month and racism awareness week! That's quite
enough. Besides new flats will create more diversity, it's the
guilt-ridden-middle-class white voters who keep me in power,
not the blacks! They don't even vote! They're too busy painting
their finger nails and getting their hair done.'

Azam picked his nails for the third time and doodled on the
council headed blue note paper, with his fifty-pound gold
engraved pen.

He scanned the council chamber and stopped. Bit his lip.
Raised an eyebrow.

'What," he mumbled under his breath, "what are they doing
here?!"

He frowned again and adjusted himself on his seat. But he
couldn't get comfortable.

"Damn," he mumbled under his breath. Dropping his pen, he
shuffled off his seat, just as councillor Davis, a dowdy looking
man, was in mid sentence about the incremental rise in the cost
of yellow bin liners.

Azam looked back, "take over will you," he said looking at
Davis, "I mean do carry on."

Davis composed himself and then continued.

"What's going on here," Flex said, looking at the proceedings
and nudging Michael, "who is this guy (looking at Abdul)? Do
you know him?"

"I thought so," Michael replied.

Abdul smiled.

Meanwhile Flex had lost all interest and was eyeing up the
female usher and rubbing his bald-head like Daddy Cool.

Azam Khan brusquely sat next to Mrs Hasim.

"What are you doing here?" Azam mumbled, looking all around
nervously.

"I've always wondered where you work Azam," she replied.

"Well now you know. Are you staying for long?"

"Hello Uncle," Misbah said smiling.

"Hello dear," he replied, looking even more guiltily around.

"You know she looks more and more like you every day," Mrs
Hasim said and "the boy Abdul, he's got a lot of your ways.
He's a real ladies' man though but thinks I don't notice."

"Mrs Hasim, what exactly do you want?"

"As you know for myself since my husband left, I've not asked for anything. But my son wants something. Can you help?"

"I'll do what I can," Azam replied.

"No Azam. I said, can you help?"

Azam nodded.

"He's at the back there. See him?"

Azam nodded.

"Then I think we'll be off and let Uncle get on with his work. (to Misbah). Take care dear."

Mrs Hasim and Misbah made a surprisingly dignified exit.

Azam wiped his forehead; it was glistening with sweat, which was turning his collar yellow. His robes seemed awkward and heavy on him now and he felt out of place.

His awkwardness turned to a feeling of ridiculousness, as he walked around the rear of the council chamber to where Abdul was standing.

Tayo and the others sat bemused and intrigued.

Abdul was waiting for him, "how are you uncle? Father sends his regards. You know keeping up appearances and that. Tower Hamlets is a small community. News travels fast."

"I understand. What is it you want?"

"Some love would be good."

"You seem to have done well without it."

"Alright then and it won't be the last time I come either. You know that vacant lot?"

"Yes, I think I know what you mean, on the hill past East Dulwich."

"Well I want you to give it to them."

"Who.... them? Those three black guys?"

"That's right."

"Why are you associating with such people?"

"Never mind about that."

"Why are you doing this? Why do you care what they want?"

"I don't!! I only care because you care so much. I know you want that land to build flats on. You'll probably make a tidy sum behind the scenes won't you! Well I want you to give it to them, you're not going to make a penny."

"You're mistaken boy, if you think I've got that much power. I'm an Asian Mayor in a majority white council. I'm fighting for my life!"

"I know that's what you say and even sometimes convince yourself. But you and I know that's not the truth. You always get what you want. You and I know that. You're a very resourceful man. That's the one thing we both have in common."

"Alright boy, I'll do what I can."

"No you'll do better than that!"

"But anyway they're going to need big money to get going."

"Let them worry about that. That's not my job or yours. You just do what I've asked."

Azam nodded. Abdul bounced out.

Azam walked towards Tayo and the others, "Can I speak to you three gentleman for a moment."

They all looked at each other, "Sure," Tayo piped up.

They stood in the corridor, Azam perturbed, looked at their baldheads nervously, "I understand you want that vacant lot," he said.

"Yes."

"What are you going to do with it?"

"You know!! We must have submitted a thousand applications!"

"Okay, but where 's your money?"

"That's not your job. You let us worry about that," Flex replied.

Azam laughed.

"Why are you laughing?" Michael said.

"Nothing," Azam smirked. He paused. "Alright, it's yours. You can leave now. Leave it in my hands. Just try and make sure it doesn't end up as a white elephant."

"I don't know what you're into," Tayo said smiling, "but I'm not, nor ever have been into white elephants."

Strange bedfellows

Dionne Douglass looked at the church full to the brim with
expectation, hope, fear, starched suits and cheap perfume.

Her mother had dragged her there. Her mother was worried.
"What happened to you was bad," her mother said, "but there's
no need to hate the whole World."

'It's strange,' Dionne thought, 'my mother talks of hate. Just
when I'm getting used to love.'

But her mother was nervous, she could see her bloodline
disappearing down the plughole, "You used to be so pretty with
your long hair and so ambitious. Now you look like a boy. Your
hair looks dreadful, when are you going to do something with
it?"

Worst still Dionne worked in a library now, no more power
dressed boardroom meetings. Her mother could not boast about
her daughter's money or job.

"What was my father like?" Dionne would ask frequently, her
questions always had a pertinent edge to them now.

"A bastard!" Her mother replied.

Dionne stared like an angel in hell and felt the flames singe her
wings.

'I love my mum,' she thought, 'But you're just part of the
problem. Why didn't you tell me the World was like this!'

And now her mother sat in church, sucking on a sweet and
playing with the brim of her ridiculously large white hat, which
sat ceremoniously on her lap.

Dionne sighed and frowned, 'I haven't felt like going to church since...never again. It wasn't just that. But what a fool I've been. I've been chasing somebody else's dream, now I'm chasing my own reality.'

Dionne looked at the decorated stained glass windows with the blonde image of Saint Maurice and another of Saint Augustine. She sighed again and looked at the rows of brown faces like children waiting for answers.

A whirlwind of emotions and thoughts crossed her mind all at once, like the electrical impulses from mother earth sent up from her womb into the heart of the earth and cascaded to the World as divine light. Dionne washed herself in the light and allowed it to permeate her inner core.

She was on her feet before she realised what she was doing.

The whole church was staring at her.

The preacher stopped.

The orchestral music stopped.

Dionne's mother opened her mouth and stared. Her dentures almost fell out, "What are you doing?!" she spat.

"I don't know, but I can't sit down," Dionne replied, her feet went straight down into the centre of the earth and her wings clipped the outer reaches of the heavens and still kept growing, she flapped them and the World moved with her.

The Pastor stared down from his pulpit, "Young lady, aren't you Ms Douglass. How can I help you my poor unfortunate child? We need to start the service."

"This service can't go on!" Dionne said, staring at the all black congregation and looking back into the Pastor's blue eyes, "it's wrong!"

"What exactly is wrong?" the Pastor said, adjusting his tie and staring down at her. His face was pale irritation, but he ironed out the creases in his forehead with false affability.

"This is not slavery!" Dionne said.

Her mother put her hands over her face with embarrassment.

"I know it's not my dear. That was a terrible crime perpetrated on your people. But in a way it was God's punishment for your pagan idolatry. But now you are closer to God. And God does work in mysterious ways."

"That's just what I mean!" Dionne continued, "I don't believe this!"

"Will you sit down," Mrs Douglass muttered, pulling on her daughter's sleeve. But her daughter's wings were flapping on the edge of her perception.

"No I've been sitting for far too long. It's time I did some standing," Dionne said and she was in the centre of the universe.

"What exactly do you want Miss Douglass? You are holding up these proceedings. I understand your pain. We are all sympathetic to what you've been through. We know what our poor sick white brother did to you. It was unforgivable! Our sister, your mother has told us everything, but that's no reason why we should all suffer."

Dionne looked at her mother with disdain, "first of all my

mother shouldn't be telling you my business, and second of all," she looked at the congregation, "he's not my brother. He may be yours'!" She looked at the Pastor and his face went ashen. His hands clammed up and he wiped his forehead. "I just want to know," Dionne continued, "how can you all sit there and pray to that?" She pointed at the image of Jesus on the wall, his blonde hair cascading across his milky white complexion and his blue eyes staring.

The congregation gasped. Mrs Douglass shook her head in disbelief.

 "Be careful young lady. What you're saying is bordering on blasphemy. Be very careful. I think the whole congregation agrees that it's time you sit down!"

There was a resounding clap from the audience.

"I don't care what they think," Dionne said staring at the Pastor, "they're your slaves!"

"My slaves???" the Pastor burbled, "**I don't know who's been brainwashing you!!**"

 "You talk to me about brainwashing, look at this, an all black congregation and an all white pastor, saints and even God all white. Just tell me who is heaven for? Tell me how is this place, this situation possible, without four hundred years of brainwashing? How did you get these black people to take you as their God, when you ain't nothing but a swindler? And I know what you're doing with my mother. And what you've been doing for years!"

Mrs Douglas stood up and flounced out, leaving her wide brimmed hat on her chair.

"I know most of you swear to be holier than thou," Dionne continued unperturbed, "but you ain't. If it's not him you're screwing (pointing to the Pastor) then it's him (pointing at Pastor John)." Pastor John was a wormy looking man with a sadistic smile on his face. He adjusted his glasses and peered with green eyes at the crowd like nothing was actually happening. He coughed, shrugged his shoulders and stared blankly.

"You are all screwing them and your husbands are all out screwing everybody else! And you all try and pretend like nothing is really happening. Do your children really know who their father is? You talk about spirituality and really you live a lie. Jesus wasn't white and all those saints aren't white either."

"It doesn't matter what colour our saviour was?" Ms Thomas piped up (she was just fresh from throwing her son Tyronne Thomas out onto the street, he was taking crack, with no prospects or ambition. 'Such a shame, I had high hopes for him.') She had been a loyal member of the church for over thirty years and these rantings were making her feel physically sick. (Ironic, because her son, twelve miles away, was vomiting for his life on a disused street corner.)

"If it doesn't, then why did you make him white in the first place?" Dionne interjected, smiling.

"Have you finished young lady?"

"Yes." Dionne replied.

"Right then," the Pastor said, "let's continue with the hymn, Jesus, Jesus, let his love wash us as white as snow."

"Yes!" Dionne exclaimed, "I have finished with this circus. Here's one black woman, who won't be your slave!" And she calmly walked out. This time her head touched the clouds but her feet were firmly on the ground.

The Pastor looked at the audience, "Well the devil is alive and working hard in our community. We must work to fight it, in all its viciousness. Will you join me?"

"I heard that you bastard!" Dionne yelled, sticking her head back through the door, "One day we're going to pull you down from there, you just wait and see!"

The congregation gasped and turned to look at her.

"Don't you ever call me a devil!" she continued, "if there's anyone here who's a devil, it's you! You fake foolin' around, fraudulent, sweaty slimy, foul smelling, lying, pickpocket potentate." She smiled, "I leave you for a while. One love." And she disappeared again through the door, bouncing with her born again spirit.

The Pastor looked up from his pulpit, opened his mouth like he was going to say something, hesitated, paused, and then changed his mind.

"Let's all join hands" Pastor John said, standing (and trying to save the day) to sing, "Jesus, blessed Jesus, wash my soul as white as snow."

The congregation waited:

Paused.

Hesitated.

They were expecting Dionne to come back for an encore. Finally, one by one, they began.

Dionne

Tayo was covered in sweat.

He ran to the top of the hill and the sun was breaking out over the hills, vales and dales. Sending cascading light over green trees, shrub, bush and everything. He stood on the edge of the greenery and watched the foliage rustling and the leaves in the autumn breeze drifting on the dew filled breeze. He sighed deep, breathing air, breath air and spirit all at once and watched the earth spinning on its axis.

Tayo cleared the hill and leapt the fence and ditch like a superman, fighting for truth, justice and freedom, in the good old African way. He skipped down a nearby embankment. The mud on his trainers slipped off on the tarmac and he trundled down faster and faster, pushing himself and extending his arms like a human windmill.

He saw a church nestling in the trees and he slipped between a nearby alcove, slipping onto the green, he skirted around the church spire, almost tripped, skipped and drove toward the hill, wiped the sweat from his face for a third time and almost bounced into Dionne going in the opposite direction.

"Sorry sista," Tayo said, smiling, as the sweat ran down his face and soaked his back.

"Don't worry about it," she replied gracefully, looking at the pools of sweat running from his face and for a fleeting moment, wondering what the sweat looked like on the rest of his body. She blushed, concealed it and blushed again.

"Well are you okay?" Tayo said, looking her up and down and a little too keenly.

"Okay, yeah I'm okay."

"Sorry, I almost knocked you over."

"It's okay, I'll survive. I'm tougher than that," and for a moment her light was blindingly sublime.

"So I see," Tayo said, sweating some more and this time staring at her all over, "you've just come from church?"

"You know you're really staring!" Dionne said.

"I know," Tayo said smiling, "do you mind? It's just when you run, your hormones go through the roof."

"That's the worst excuse I've ever heard. But at least you're up front," she said and thought again about him sweating all over, she frowned at her own audacity.

"Why are you frowning?" Tayo said shaking out his legs and stretching.

"Nothing," Dionne replied looking at him bending over and feeling the perspiration break out on **her** forehead. She was shining like the moon.

"You almost look as hot as me," Tayo said looking at her flushing.

"No I'm alright," she said, collecting her thoughts and licking her lips.

"So you've just been to church," Tayo said again, almost sneering.

"Not really, but kind of" and she smiled like an angel, sitting on the moon, "and why did you change the subject?"

"What?" Tayo said, trying to read her and not succeeding.

"Never mind. Anyway have a good day," she said and turned to leave.

Tayo looked at the ground, "wait, what's your name?"

"Dionne," she replied.

"So what were you doing in there?"

"It's a long story."

"I 'm glad anyway, that's no place for a decent African," and he walked away.

"Hey," Dionne replied, running after him and almost tripping on the grass, "you didn't tell me your name?"

"It's Tayo."

"Really, it's better than Steve anyway!"

"What!?"

"Nothing."

"I mean what do you do?"

"I run into women who go to church and then ask them out."

"I mean it seriously?"

"So do I."

"Listen, you seem like a nice guy, but I've been going through some bad times recently. I'm really not ready for anything serious," she said, staring at his crotch and almost convincing herself!

"I'm sorry, I didn't mean to offend you. Well, to be honest, I gave up my high powered job some months ago and I'm working to develop this Black project."

"Really," she said and thinking, 'it's like our lives were parallel and we didn't even know it.'

"Yeah, but you know it's nothing but a struggle."

"Black project. What's it going to be called?"

"I don't know, but it's going to do a lot of good anyway. Have you been around recently on the buses and the trains, people are starving. They're starving for knowledge!"

"I'm sure, listen, put me on your mailing list or something."

"What's your email?"

"Lostfoundlove21@hotmail.com"

"That's good," Tayo said, "I can't forget that," and he skipped away. Dionne looked at his ass until he disappeared up the hill.

'Shame on you,' she thought, 'just looking at a brother as a sex object. That can't work' and then she smiled. That was the first time since him, that she had even allowed herself to have those kind of thoughts. And she chuckled to herself, 'Tayo, nice name. Tayo nice bum!'

Drinking on the job

Steve was stoned out of his head. He missed the first step and
slid on to the second, staggered and looked up at the World.
The sky seemed a daze. The clouds grey black against the
greying sky raced after each other, consuming and being
consumed. The moon looked a blur, as clouds swallowed her
whole, again and again.

Steve stumbled across the street, missing a parked car and
dodging an oncoming one. He coughed the contents of his
stomach up on the pavement and part of it dripped onto a
nearby railing. He stumbled towards the tube entrance and
deposited himself on the top of the stairs.

"Bloody hell, I'm bladdered," he mumbled, "I've had a
skinfull."

He vomited again, slipped and finally sat in it, like a pig in his
sh....

Tayo was early for his meeting. He skipped along the pavement
like a very good boxer who had just won a very long fight. He
almost tripped over Steve who lay sprawled on the street.

"Sorry," Tayo said bluntly.

"What you bastard!" Steve mumbled.

"Pardon?" Tayo replied.

"I called you a black bastard!"

Tayo smiled and laughed, "you're drunk and I'm busy."

"Not.. drunk... enough to take on the likes... of you!"

"Now before you do, what I think your going to do. You'd better think twice."

Steve stared at him like a rare endangered animal in a cage.

"What?"

"I said," Tayo replied, "do we have to do this?"

Tayo turned to walk away.

Steve grabbed a bottle and leapt after him lunging. The air rushed past and the leaves rustled in the trees. A Black Cat stood on a white wall and pissed on it.

Tayo ducked and kicked Steve in his head.

Steve wiped the blood and vomit from his mouth and he picked up a broken stick.

"Don't," Tayo scowled and his forehead creased up.

Steve feinted and swung wildly, Tayo kicked him twice, the last time in his head and he rolled and swung back a glancing blow. But Steve kept coming. Swinging with his fists, (he'd dropped the stick in the former melee), it clipped Tayo's chin. 'The power lays not in the hand, it is in what controls the hand,' Tayo thought, swerving and punching back, an uppercut to the ribs, weaving past a bevy of Steve's hastily concocted punches.

Tayo stood at the edge of the steps and looked down the dark tunnel beneath. Avoiding a brick thrown his way, he kneed Steve in his chest and elbowed him in the jaw, grabbing Steve around the neck, and yanked him down the stairs.

Steve skipped the first.

His heels clipped the second.

His shoulder grazed the third

And his head hit the fourth.

Tayo leapt after him, driving his heels into Steve's ribs and kidneys, the blood trickled out and dribbled down the steps. Steve attempted to stand up. Tayo kneed him in his chest again and this time Steve just lay there.

Tayo smirked, looking at Steve's injuries and he walked briskly and calmly by, pulling down the sleeves of his coat. And he thought, 'understand the nature of all things. If you grab a stinging nettle firmly it cannot sting you. If you treat it like a flower, you'll be hurt.'

Steve came to. He was at the bottom of the steps leading to Elephant and Castle tube station and he couldn't move. He lay in a pool of his own blood and he mumbled, "this.... can't... be happening... not to me... not now." The gun that was in his pocket slipped out and fell underneath his belly. He rolled on it and pushed it into the gutter. He looked around so that no one could see. And he lay there.

At his Convenience

"Lis...ten..... he...... w..as.... bl...ac...k..." Steve mumbled, his jaw was broken in three places (and he now deeply regretted that he had not shot him.)

"I heard what you said the first time," the policeman replied, staring at Steve as he lay there in the hospital bed. "But we've already had reports that earlier in the day you had been drunk and abusive to a number of people," the policeman added.

"Do.....ctor.... Doc...tor," Steve mumbled.

"Listen just keep your mouth shut and rest," the policeman added. "Listen we looked into your account of what happened and it doesn't ring true. There's a camera just above where you say the fight took place and it didn't catch a damn thing! Frankly, we've heard that some people want to press charges against you for your behaviour!"

"Yo...u're bl..o..ody j...ok..ing!"

"Do I look like I'm joking? I think you should speak to a lawyer and soon."

"Th..at's r...idi..cu...lous, lo..o..k a..t t..h.e, s.. t..a.te of m.e.. Th.i.s is s..t.i.ll my cou....ntry i.n. it???!"

"Pardon?"

"I.. m..e...an I. s...t..ill h...ave.. r..ig..hts d..on't I???!!."

"Yeah like I said you need to be speaking to a lawyer."

"Im...po..ss...ible, fe...tch me a p..hone!"

"Sure."

"Lis....ten ca...n y..ou d..ial t.he n....um..ber f.or m.e, 0204 222 1122. J...ust hold the re...ceive..r ne...xt to my e...ar."

The dial of the phone rang and there was a click as the receiver was picked up.

"He....llo And...rew, And...rew Som.e.rset, th...is i.s St...eve, lis...ten I n..eed y..our h..elp. I...'m i..n hos...pital, so..me hod...lum att..ac..ked m......e, it's a b..ig me....ss. The...re's po..lice he...re and every.....thing."

On the other end of the receiver, there was a long pause. Finally, "Listen I don't know who you are? But don't ever, ever, call me again! Do you understand?" The line went dead.

"Happy now," the policeman said putting the receiver back on the phone and smiling like a cat.

"You bas....tard, yo.....u've all sti...tc....hed m...e u.p."

"Listen you're in no position to be getting excited. They'll be plenty of time for that. And like I said you'd better get yourself a good solicitor."

Steve frowned. He would have clenched his fists, but they hurt too much.

"Blood......y ro.....tten coun....try," he mumbled.

"Don't you dare talk badly about my country!" the policeman said staring at him,"listen if you've got nothing else to say, we'll see you tomorrow. And you'd better start thinking about your statement."

The policeman undid the flap of his pocket and put his
notebook in it, with the clinical efficiency of an executioner.

He turned his back on Steve and strode off, each calculated step
hardly touching the floor.

Steve coughed, mumbled and finally resorted to wetting his
bed. It was his last act of defiance. He smiled as he lay in his
own piss, but he was beside himself with rage.

Hits

Michael flicked on the Radio.

"It is now 10pm and this is the news," burbled from the speakers.

Michael sat down in his favourite chair.

"Former Iraqi President Saddam Hussein has been executed by hanging in Baghdad. An Iraqi court sentenced him and two co-defendants to death. Leaders in Iraq and beyond, as well as representatives of non-governmental organisations, have been giving their reactions."

"Tragedy in Spain. A bomb exploded in the parking lot of Terminal 4 of Barajas Airport, Madrid, Spain, killing two people and damaging cars and buildings. We have a special report to follow and we go to the Spanish community in England for reactions. We have established a special hotline for people who may be worried."

"Former U.S. President Gerald Ford's funeral is held at the United States Capitol. We go for a report later in this show. As condolences come from across the World, we will be talking to his family about the contribution that he made to the development of America."

"A 67-year-old Spanish woman, whose name has not been revealed, is reported to have given birth to twins in Barcelona, she is the oldest birth mother."

"The coat of arms of Nepal is changed today as a gesture of reconciliation after the Nepalese Civil War."

"At least 500 people are feared to have drowned after the ferry

Senopati Nusantara travelling between the port of Kumai on the Indonesian island of Borneo to Semarang on Java sank during a storm. But none of them were Europeans and there were no Britons among the dead."

"In other news, in Africa, the Congo forces of renegade General Laurent Nkunda and the UN-backed army clashed in North Kivu province, prompting some 50,000 people to flee. The UN Security Council expresses concern about the fighting. As many as 5,000 people are feared dead. But none of them were Europeans and there were no Britons among the dead."

"Finally in Africa, in Somalia, at the Battle of Jilib, the ICU frontlines collapsed during the night to artillery fire, causing the ICU to retreat, abandoning Kismayo without a fight and retreating towards the Kenyan border. Many thousands are feared dead, but no westerners and no Britons are among the dead."

Michael sighed, 'is one man's death more important than many? Who judges the value of a man's life? Are our lives really less important than their's. That can't be right!' He turned the radio off in disgust, adjusted his glasses and clicked on his computer. 'You have two hundred hits,' it read. 'Well someone out there agrees with us,' he thought.

Revelations II

Tayo stood outside the bus stop giving out fliers. There were
rats everywhere, gorging themselves on the city's waste.
Eastern Europeans flooded the Ghetto, knocking obsolete
blacks to the kerb and kicking them there. The first sprightly
bouncing, with the vim and vigour of success - whilst the latter
trudged, scuffing, picking up cigarette butts or floated with
corporate sponsered chains and wide indifferent falsehoods,
false hair, false suits and false faces: scattered, intergrated, lost
and bemused, drunk on the liqour of a king's lullaby.

Tayo's hands were cold and he was fed up. But he thought,
'When the sun and moon shine with each other, I'll shine with
them. When the snow and rain falls I never falter. I've made a
promise that I'd go on to the end - come rain or shine, never
mind what the World brings. Now that the rain is falling more
than it did. I promise I'm goin' to stay with this to the end,' and
he sighed.

"We always thought you were going to make a difference."

Tayo spun round half expecting to see Michael or Flex. They
were late.

Instead, a rather well but not over dressed man, with polished
teeth was talking into his mobile phone.

"Oh no! I wasn't talking to you, (looking at Tayo) sorry, you
just can't get the staff these days."

Tayo half nodded and looked him up and down. There was
something in the man's spirit that he just couldn't read,
something stubborn, strong and very, very, persistent.

Tayo looked away, 'Where are they?' and he scanned the street for Flex and Michael.

"Yeah I thought you were going to make a difference."

Tayo looked up and round again.

The man smiled at him, his head pressed into the phone, his blonde hair almost white against the evening moon.

Tayo half turned back.

"Yeah," the man said. He walked nearer to Tayo. Tayo could smell his exceptionally expensive deodorant and it stank.

"Yes, listen, I'm not prejudiced at all. I think you're doing an important job! Listen there's room for all varieties of leadership. If we'd wanted you gone, you'd be gone already. In fact I have high hopes for you. You just need a little direction. Anyway I can't stay on the phone for long." He flipped his phone shut.

Tayo turned around once more and stared at him.

The man smiled again, "You know people these days" (to Tayo).

"I blame the schools," Tayo said mocking and looking into his blue eyes.

"Do you?" The man said intently, "interesting."

"Anyway take care," (to Tayo) "I think I'm late. What was your name?" he extended his manicured fingernails.

"Tayo," Tayo said, half shaking his hand and feeling in that hand, the almost insurmountable weight of white supremacy, fully confident, ambivalent, transparently versatile, adaptable and organic.

"Anyway take care," the man said.

"What's your name?" Tayo called to him.

"Oh my name is Andrew. Andrew Somerset, take care Ta..Yo!" and he strode confidently away.

Tayo watched him go and his shadow moved across the surface of the earth. It combined by osmosis with everything, the teeth of a pet dog being dragged across the street, the silver thread on an old Sikh man's turban as he walked along the road. The white plastic on the shoes of a baby being pushed in her pram. The yellow lettering on the bold sports logo of a careless youth, with his trousers down by his ankles. This man's shadow was in everything.

Michael bounced up the steps, and the shadow seemed to dissipate a little, but then it expanded and retracted around him like a coil, settling beneath the cracks in the pavement. Michael looked at his watch. "Sorry I'm late, there was untold problems on the Northern line. They held us at the station for half an hour. This place feels odd."

"Yeah I know what you mean, you know I had the strangest conversation," Tayo said, "Have you seen Flex?"

"No he just sent me a text he can't make it, he's been held up. And I know what you mean about conversations. I've been having ones all week. It must be something in the air," Michael said straightening his tie.

Tayo reached inside his bag and pulled out some leaflets, "we'd better start then," and Michael stood at the street corner with leaflets in hand and they smiled at women and men frowned at them.

"Is this working?" Tayo said.

"You know my view on all this." Michael replied.

"Don't say it, n.... have got to die. After all these years is that the best you can come up with?"

"In fact, what I was going to say is that this type of work has a role, but the most important thing is to diversify our methods. We need roots in every sector of our society and we need to exploit every method known."

"You're right."

"And we should pay someone to do this job, whilst we do something else."

"Yeah all right." Tayo said, packing up his leaflets. "Well you think of a concrete plan and we'll meet at 7am tomorrow and put it into execution, is that fair?"

"Alright."

That night...

Michael sat in his spacious office loft, in his five-bedroom house and smiled at his handy work, flow charts and diagrams, illustrations and cumulative indexes. But then he frowned and rested his head on his hands.

'No plan no matter how perfect, ever survives the first encounter with the enemy. After all,' Michael thought, 'we're dealing with our people. What seems logical is usually illogical. Use the mind, but let the spirit direct it and he started to work again.'

Dreams

Next day

"I had my first decent dream in sixteen years," Flex said staring at Michael and Tayo.

"Yeah what happened?" Tayo replied.

"I was standing outside this place. I mean it could have been our building. But it was pitch dark. And I couldn't even see my own hand. I mean it was that dark. And I was looking for this key, but I really couldn't find it. Then it was strange. You two arrived. I didn't feel lost anymore. But there was still something missing. We needed this key but none of us had it. And it was pitch dark."

"Then this woman drives up from nowhere. Yes that's right some strange woman. She came in this strange car and jumps out. I understand you've been looking for this key she says. We all look at each other really relieved and excited. And she goes, how're you going to make this work without women. We all sort of looked at each other again and then there's a silence and then two more women appear and we look at each other again and then all six of us get in this car. I don't know how we do it. But we do."

"Then this woman says, oh but we forgot something. So we all get out and the sun is coming up in a nearby field. There's an old tyre in a field. And it starts to move - I mean the tyre. We are all six of us looking at this old tyre and underneath it this huge frog comes out. I mean it's green and black with these little red eyes. And it sort of leaps out onto the road in front of us. We all stare at each other again. The Sun is really shining now."

"And one of us wants to stamp on this frog. But you - yes you Tayo say no! Don't it's a sign, a very good sign!"

"This frog looks at us and keeps crawling through the undergrowth and there's like this bundle attached to its hind legs. Yes there's a bundle and the frog deposits this bundle on the roadside."

"We all look and what comes bursting out is a baby. His eyes are Black, coal Black, the iris, pupil and cornea all Black and this baby sort of crawls out of the undergrowth and over the frog. It walks past us and gets into this car that we've just been in and sits down in the front seat."

"The baby turns around and looks at us and says, "by the way I'm Hope." And his chest lights up where his heart is. Then the strange thing is. All our chests light up and you can see the letters hope there and then we all get in this car."

"You mean," Tayo says, "we're only half way through. We've got to find these three women in your dream. Somehow, I feel each of us along our road know who these people are."

"I'm sure one is Susan," Michael said.

"But where 's Susan?" Tayo interjected.

"I heard she's in the Congo and owns some massive plantation, she's really rich." Michael added.

"So," Flex said, "we'd better start looking."

The Morning sun 2007 style

Michael sat in the morning sun of a new year and watched the
sun drenched horizon appear crescent across the sky. He had
taken to having early walks to catch the sunrise. It was three
miles from where he lived to the place. Their place, their field
of dreams but now in reality a set of derelict buildings.

He sat.

'I was not so keen on this idea at first,' he thought, 'but now if
we don't succeed at this, I don't know what I'll do,' he thought.
A tear almost formed itself on his left eye and though he tried
to convince himself it wasn't there. It just grew and grew until
he sat there weeping, not for himself or pride, thwarted
ambition, the pangs of rejected love. Michael's tears were for
all the children that would be born with half a heart and half a
lung, because this place, their place did not exist.

He wept when he thought of the Malika's and their pain.
'Malika, could she be one.' He wept for all the children on the
buses and the tubes. 'Could any of those people be fundamental
to this cause?' He wept for the little boys fed on the breast of
gangster materialism and he wept for the girls born from the
womb of selfish indifference. He wept and his face was soaked
in tears.

'The nightmare of my reality seems so close,' he thought and he
kept crying like a baby.

Dionne had been investigating the circle of life now since Tayo
had spoken to her.

She logged on and watched, as their website expanded its
appeals and developed its programmes. 'There is evidence of
professionalism and astute business minds, she would say, as

each new development took place. They've got their legal matters tight and their budget plans,' she thought, 'but they lack something.'

She realised, 'there are no women. No women working with them at all. And they don't have enough money!' She saw through all their ideas. 'There is an air of desperation and a resignation of failure. They've put their last money in, but they haven't received enough financial support. They're on their last legs,' and she sighed, as she looked at their Web Pages and rested her chin on her hands. She looked now with greater eagerness and intent.

And now she walked as she did most mornings, but with less fear through the streets of South London. She knew where she was going.

There was air in her step, though it was 7am and she didn't know what to expect, until she got there. It had taken her forty minutes, following the maps on the internet and she stood at the bottom of the hill and looked up

And now she walked, forwards ever, backwards never and up that hill. She studied her maps, 'what am I doing?' she thought many times, as the sun wasn't even fully risen and the morning dew was still wet. But she climbed undaunted. And she finally felt the breeze of the air near the summit. The air was still. She walked and then stopped.

She heard the sound of tears, not those of a child or a woman which are relatively common, but those of a man and a mannish man too.

She stopped and stared.

And assuming it was Tayo's baldhead, she crept closer.

Michael turned and stared.

"Sorry," she said, "I thought you were somebody else," and she turned to leave, suddenly embarrassed and a little bit afraid. After all it was 7am in the half-light on an isolated hill, in the middle of South London. Surely this was not ideal for a single woman by herself!

But Michael smiled and her fears subsided, "It's alright," he said, "I don't make a habit of it."

"Even if you did, would it be a problem?"

Michael smiled again, "well."

"I came here looking for someone else."

Michael looked.

"His name is..." she said.

"Tayo," Michael answered.

"How did you know? Do you know him?"

The sun was just coming up over the horizon and spreading its orange red light across the sky. The light and life of the World was tingling with the anticipation of a new day.

"In a way Tayo is my brother and I'm his."

"Yeah I see the resemblance, you know the head."

Michael smiled.

"Are you working on this project? " she continued. "You know for here - for this place, there's really nothing up here - no sign or anything to say that you own it and work is being done."

"If only you knew. By the way my name is Michael. And yours is?"

"Dionne," she said, "I don't know why but I trust you. Though you're sitting on a hill at 7am crying your eyes out. But then why am I here? That's pretty illogical isn't it? I haven't got much time. But I want you to do something for me. I don't carry a chequebook or anything like that, but trust me when I say this, I have already deposited £80,000 in your project. It's not a grant, it's a loan and I want it back with interest. There are a lot of papers to sign when you next go into your bank, you'll see. But I just had to see this place."

The Sun was radiant and the trees shook with light and life and healing breath, even though the wind picked up a little and rattled them.

Michael said nothing but stared.

"Aren't you going to speak?"

"What words! No this is beyond words, let's just watch the view."

And they sat arm in arm and watched the Sun spread its raiment over the earth and filter its subtle, persuasive power over and into everything.

The Parade

False vengeance rode through the town in red, white and blue,
Waving his flag and singing a patriotic tune,
With slip on shiny shoes and a stupid pompous walk,
With a sharp suit and a politically correct remark.
Killing and smiling and lying and killing!
Stamping on human hearts, forever and ever.
Next came materialism, greed and contempt,
They skanked and they fronted and sometimes even shouted,
But it was all a game,
Though they sucked and blew the light from the earth and spat
out darkness instead.
Then came ignorance high on a horse, in a veil of conceit,
He ate all their hopes;
While mothers wept to be pleasured by his pain,
Offering their children for his dinner table.
The Boys yelled with glee when chaos stepped up,
The lord of mode, player of games, and master of lies,
He led the people on a merry dance for nothing and to nowhere
and for no reason at all.
Then came apathy, lord of the ceremonies and king of the hill,
He lolloped in his own filth and looked like a clown,
Smiling like a devil and wearing a crumbling crown.

And the soul of man cried.....,where is my mind!!???

But there in the square, dressed all in black was Hope and she
cried,
I'm goin' to make you love me!
Half her face was a woman as black as midnight
and the..
the other half ...
the other half was Tayo's.

Tayo woke in a cold sweat, sheets all adrift, with only the pale
moon for light, with *apathy* and *chaos* triumphant and rampant,
towers of despair, ghastly pale grey in the pitched night. But in
the midst of Tayo's profound spiritual eloquence, with the
utmost absolute perfection of his destiny, he wrestled with
them, right there and right then, though they held him with
rasping, ghastly, cold clammy hands. He dragged them down
into the earth and his arms and hands were blessed as Black as
the centre of the universe from which the word itself was born.
He pinned them and watched, as the earth swallowed them,
impurities and all, their manufactured spiritual filth dying with
their demise and he did it with absolute love. And he was
blessed again and again and again......

Susan typed

Susan realised as she looked at the soul of the sun, 'white supremacy has been pouring the blood of self hate into the heart of every African man, woman and child in every street, town and city, in every part of the World. There will always be a messenger to tell me the World is bleeding and I can't stop the blood by smiling at the Sun. No it will take more than that to stop the blood!'

Susan typed into her computer, as she watched the **Sun** dying behind the African horizon, 'I know it's been over ten years, but I've got to come **home.** There's been some strange things happening which tell me, I've got to come home and I'm bringing my daughter Simone with me. She's quite a woman now. I hope this is still your email address Tayo. We've got to talk.'

Tayo walked

Three days later Tayo looked at himself in the mirror and burnt a hole in the glass and he frowned because the hole wasn't big enough and then he walked. He walked through the developing foundations and the outer brickwork almost done. 'The sign will be good there,' he thought, 'Karibu Nyumba.' There on the first floor will be an internet café, on the second all the educational facilities, perhaps a drop in centre over there in the corner. Perhaps we'll sell some food there if we get a licence, shouldn't be a problem. Perhaps round the back a soup kitchen?? Who knows?'

The wind rustled through the trees in agreement and a single leaf lifted over the construction work and settled in the centre of the stone floors.

Tayo walked past a skip full of old bricks, stones, wood, crisp packets, kit-kat wrappers, and a dead rat.

He closed his eyes, as the Sun pushed its light behind his lids and into his retina, he could feel the morning light tickling his consciousness and feeding the inner light in the uppermost aspect of his central being. The lights went on. All ten of them from crown to foundation, he felt his heart beat in his fingernails and his thoughts in his feet.

He put on his hat and skipped out, taking a look one last time. This will be a place that will change people's lives. It will be a safe place.

Tayo walked onto a side street and out onto the main road. He walked past the drug dealers and they stared at him. It was early for him - but late for them. They looked at him like a low life stranger and a fool. He walked past a corporate sponsored fool, in his west end gear assimilated, with his jolly mad girl friend, drunk out of his head. It was only six am. They scowled at him. A tramp high on acid and PCP spat just in front of him. Tayo skipped around it and kept on walking.

Tyronne Thomas only nineteen years old - now addicted to crack, was down and out on the street, full of malice (for himself), his muscular thighs wasted, his smooth brown skin diseased. "Give us a pound you bastard!" he yelled. Tayo disregarded his abuse and walked on by. A truck driver almost skipped onto the sidewalk to kill him. Tayo stepped aside and missed the speeding vehicle. The driver cursed him out of the window for getting in his way. Tayo ignored him and kept going. A group of black youth stared at Tayo and muttered to themselves, one of them flicked a knife open. Tayo just kept on walking. The leaves floated all around him but didn't touch. The Sun was filtering through the cascading fauna and Tayo smiled to himself because everything was back to 'normal.'

Epilogue

Three years later..

"We cannot agree to that," Tayo said.

"It's not going to happen," Susan added.

"Listen you're all doing well. I mean it. You've done wonders. You've got all the young people in the area on your side and you've got businesses and everything. How **did** you do that?"

Silence.

"You're really doing good work. But you know you don't have any real power. You and your people must comply."

"No!" Susan said.

"What!!!!!"

"No!" Tayo reiterated, "**we** don't have to comply with anything, except the beating of our own hearts."

Read **Waiting to Explode** and **The Black Prince** by Onyeka

Website www.onyeka.co.uk